"Okay," she said with one firm up-and-down motion of their hands. "Partners."

Mark stared down at their hands. His feeble return of her handshake was nothing short of pitiful. "Partners," he muttered.

She pulled her hand out of his. Immediately he felt the coolness of the morning air on his palm, almost making him shiver with the loss of the warm contact.

Chantelle turned toward the diner. Not knowing what else to do while he tried to organize his addled brain, Mark rammed his hand into his pocket and turned as well.

"There it is," she sighed. "Joe's Diner."

GAIL SATTLER lives in Vancouver, BC (where you don't have to shovel rain) with her husband, three sons, two dogs, five lizards, and countless fish, many of whom have names. She writes inspirational romance because she loves happily-ever-afters and believes God has a place in that happy ending. Visit Gail's Web site at www.gailsattler.com.

Books by Gail Sattler

HEARTSONG PRESENTS

Joe's Diner

Gail Sattler

Heartsong Presents

Dedicated to Ryan and Mike. Ordering a hamburger and fries will never feel the same. Honorable mention goes to Kathy. Thank you.

A note from the author:
I love to hear from my readers! You may correspond with me by writing:

> **Gail Sattler**
> **Author Relations**
> **PO Box 719**
> **Uhrichsville, OH 44683**

ISBN 1-58660-765-0

JOE'S DINER

All Scripture quotations, unless otherwise indicated, are taken from the HOLY BIBLE, NEW INTERNATIONAL VERSION®. NIV®. Copyright © 1973, 1978, 1984 by International Bible Society. Used by permission of Zondervan Publishing House. All rights reserved.

All of the characters and events in this book are fictitious. Any resemblance to actual persons, living or dead, or to actual events is purely coincidental.

one

"Hi, Chantelle. How's the job hunt coming?"

Chantelle Dubois cradled the phone between her chin and her shoulder as she settled in for a good long talk with her uncle Joe. She laid her red pen down on the table and stared blankly at the *Help Wanted* section spread all over the kitchen table in front of her. "I haven't found anything yet. But there are a few promising ones today."

"Do you mind suspending your job search for awhile? I need a favor. And it's a big one."

Chantelle grasped the phone properly with one hand and turned to the calendar on the wall. If she didn't find a job within the next week, she wouldn't have enough money in her account to make her next month's rent. As it was, she'd been living on macaroni and wieners for the past week to stretch her last dollars as far as possible.

However, because her uncle Joe was asking, Chantelle suspected that, once again, he had pushed himself past his limits. Most likely, he was shorthanded and needed her to run some kind of errand that had to be done during business hours.

She really couldn't spare the day, but she couldn't turn down her favorite uncle. "What do you need?"

"It's Jack. He's had an accident."

Chantelle swallowed hard. She'd always liked her uncle's best friend and business partner. Her stomach churned as she contemplated the worst that could have happened. She struggled to speak through the lump in her throat and couldn't. Fortunately, her uncle continued without waiting for her to respond.

"Jack's car was broadsided on the way to work this morning.

Susan phoned from the hospital. She didn't say much, only that he's been hurt. It sounds pretty bad, but she says he's going to make it. Praise God for that. But the point of it is that the diner's shorthanded with no notice. Since you're still looking for a job, how about if you come and work for me until Jack is back on his feet? I'll pay you what I would pay anyone else. I don't expect you to do this for free."

Visions of her uncle's restaurant flashed through her mind. Jack and Uncle Joe had owned and operated Joe's Diner since she was a child.

Over the years, many of her cousins had worked for her uncle. For most, it had been a first job or a place to work part-time during high school or college. However, Chantelle's first job had been as a cashier for a large discount department store. After graduation from high school, she'd found various office jobs where she spent most of her time seated behind a desk.

"I don't know. I've never done that kind of thing before. Can't you ask somebody else?"

"Kevin called in sick and I gave Esther a couple of weeks off to move, so I was already shorthanded in the kitchen when Susan phoned. As to part-timers, Bob quit last week, and Jackie's not finished school. I need you, Chantelle."

His pleading tone made her squirm in her chair, so she stood to continue the conversation.

Jack did the bookkeeping, but his main functions were as head cook and kitchen manager.

Chantelle didn't like to cook, which probably explained why she wasn't good at it. Everyone knew she wasn't the most coordinated person in the world. She'd also never held a supervisory position in her life. Uncle Joe's request told her his state of desperation.

The figures of her dwindling bank account ran through her mind, as well as the speech she'd been composing to explain to her landlord why she had to, once again, write another post-dated check for the rent.

A few weeks, as he said, wouldn't ease her money worries, but it would pay the next month's rent on time.

Chantelle checked her watch. By now, the restaurant had opened, and with Jack's absence, things would already be backing up.

"Okay, I'll do it. I'll be there in half an hour."

☙

"I'm so sorry, Uncle Joe! I don't know how the lid fell off like that. At least it was only sugar. I'll sweep it up."

Her uncle shook his head and smiled, but she could tell he was trying to be polite. "Make sure you do a thorough job. All foodstuffs are kept in sealed containers because we can't attract bugs. We'll have to power-wash the floor tonight instead of the usual mopping or we'll get ants. But we'll worry about that later. For now, I'll go into the locker for another bag. The orders are backing up. Make sure you're not burning those eggs."

Without another word, he spun on his toes and hurried down the stairs.

Chantelle held her breath while she frantically grabbed the flipper, removed the eggs in question from the grill, and laid them onto the waiting plates. She wiped the sweat off her brow with the corner of her apron, then pressed the accompanying pieces of bacon down with the flipper to help them cook faster, hopefully before the eggs got too cold to serve to waiting customers. "I'll have this ready in a minute," she called out to Brittany, who was not very patiently waiting at the pickup counter.

She managed to get through the lunch rush with slightly less difficulty than breakfast. However, by the time the supper period was in full swing, she had passed her maximum level of efficiency and started on a downward spiral.

Even though it was Thursday and the restaurant wasn't busy, she somehow mixed up a couple of orders. She'd also accidentally sprinkled sugar instead of salt on someone's fries. She didn't mean to spill the gravy on the stack of dishes as they came out of the dishwasher, and she certainly hadn't meant to drop the frying pan on Uncle Joe's foot when he unexpectedly appeared beside her. After burning a couple of hamburgers, she decided to time everything using the alarm on her wristwatch. It wasn't her fault that spending extra attention to get the hamburgers right slowed down everything else.

By the latter part of the evening, Chantelle could finally relax. The only things she had to worry about amounted to serving the odd order of fries, cutting up fancy cakes and pies, and making sure to start a fresh pot of coffee every twenty minutes or so. After just one day in the restaurant business, she confirmed in her mind, body, heart, and soul that, when she resumed her job search, she would definitely not be seeking employment as a short-order cook.

Finally, Uncle Joe unplugged the neon OPEN sign, signaling to the outside world that the restaurant was closed for the day. When Uncle Joe locked up behind the last customers as they left, Chantelle sagged against the wall, barely keeping herself from sinking to the floor.

"Okay, everyone! Time to clean up! It's been a tough day, and I appreciate all your extra work. Chantelle, you can start with sweeping up, and then give the kitchen a quick mop. Dave, you power-wash after she's done. And Chantelle, when I'm done doing the deposit, we need to talk."

Numbly, Chantelle nodded. If her boss for the day had been anyone other than her uncle, she knew, rather than going into paid overtime, she would have been fired right after mistaking the ice bin for a trash compactor. Still, the words she knew her uncle was going to say echoed through her head as she cleaned up the mess, most of which she'd either made or caused to some degree.

"I'm sorry, I know you tried your best, but this isn't going to work."

"I'm sorry, I should never have asked you to do this."

"I'm sorry, but I'm going to have to find someone else."

With every response rehearsed in her head, she, too, started with "I'm sorry." She couldn't wait for her uncle. To spare her uncle the difficulty of having to fire her, Chantelle walked into his office and shut the door behind her as soon as she finished mopping.

"I'm so sorry, Uncle Joe. I've made such a mess of things today. I'm really not cut out for this."

He nodded as he entered some numbers into the computer. "I know. Don't forget that you've had to work more than a regular eight-hour shift, too. I know that's hard, especially for the first time you've done this. So I've decided to move Evelyn into the kitchen and have you do serving. I think I've got a uniform or two that will fit you."

Chantelle blinked and sank into the chair in front of his desk. "Pardon me?"

"I shouldn't have put you in the kitchen when you didn't have any experience. That was my mistake, and I'm sorry. I hope I haven't turned you off to restaurant work for the rest of your life."

"You're really willing to give me another chance? You're not going to fire me?"

His hands froze over the keyboard, and he looked up at her. "Of course not. You're my niece and I love you. You came because I asked you to help me. I'm not going to fire you for an error in my own judgment." He smiled. "Besides, you can't do as bad a job as a waitress as you did as a short-order cook. Now if you're done, just punch out and go home. Before you go, pick a uniform from the back closet. I'll see you about noon."

⁂

Mark Daniels stared at the computer screen in front of him. His brain had gone blank, and he couldn't remember the next step in a simple reconciliation he'd done thousands of times.

Of course, the pounding migraine, which seemed to be a

daily occurrence, didn't help. Hoping to make the banging in his head stop, Mark leaned back in his chair, pushed his fingers into the center of his forehead, and rotated his thumbs into his temples. When massaging the pressure points failed to ease the incessant throbbing, Mark opened his desk drawer and gulped down a couple of prescription headache tablets with a sip of his cold coffee.

Hoping that refocusing his eyes on a faraway point would help to clear his mind, Mark sought a momentary distraction from the mountainous volume of work on his desk. He flexed his fingers at his sides and glanced around the room, focusing on the calendar hanging on the office wall. Instead of looking at the picture of the sports car, he studied the colored lines indicating the staff's scheduled vacations.

The only vacation not listed was his own. He had so much work he couldn't leave until he was caught up enough to take a couple weeks off.

There hadn't been a good time in two years. And now, with the ban on overtime, when someone went on vacation, the rest of the already overworked staff had to absorb the duties of the missing person. Since Mark was the supervisor, he was the only salaried employee in the department. According to the company owner, being middle management meant Mark was the one required to work until the cows came home, without being paid overtime wages. Therefore, most of the extra work ended up in his already overflowing basket filled with client files with looming deadlines, some of them already past.

"Mark? I need the McHenry file."

Mark blinked and stared blankly at the secretary, who had just stepped through the door into his office. Joanne stopped in front of his desk, expectantly waiting for him to produce the requested file, as if he knew where it was in the mountain of paper.

His chest tightened. "I don't remember that one," he mumbled.

"It's really Darren's file."

Darren, his assistant, had been off sick for a few days, but that didn't explain why Joanne thought he had the file.

Joanne glanced between all the piles on his desk. "They just phoned to say they need their last month's profit-and-loss statement completed by eight A.M. Monday."

He scanned all the piles of folders and stacks of computer disks in his office, from the four piles lined across his desk, to those stacked over the surface of his credenza, to the new pile he'd started on top of his filing cabinet. "I don't remember you giving me that file," he mumbled as he squeezed his eyes shut and again pressed his fingers into his aching temples.

"I didn't actually give it to you. You weren't at your desk, so I left a note on it and put it in the pile of the day."

Mark blinked again. He scanned each pile, trying to think of where it could be.

He arrived at the high-rise office tower to open up the office an hour before the first person started. He left many hours after everyone else, even on weekends. Every day for the past six months, he'd worked through his lunch, even though there was barely room for a sandwich and his coffee mug between his computer and the mess on his desk. The only time he was absent from his desk was when he left to use the men's room.

"What day did you leave it with me?"

"Tuesday. I think. Or was it Wednesday? Does it matter?"

Mark slid the document folder from the bottom of the first pile, then slid one out of what he thought might be the middle of the accumulation of the third pile. "Let's see. The deadline on this one was last Wednesday, and the deadline on this one is the middle of next week. So that means deadlines for Monday would be. . ." He let his voice trail off as he thumbed midway through the second pile, inching toward the direction of where he had pulled the latter file. "Here," he mumbled as he pulled out the McHenry file.

As soon as he saw the note attached, which outlined the extent of what needed to be done, he saw himself once again working until two in the morning in order to meet one more critical deadline.

Something in his chest tightened. At age thirty-two, he figured he was probably too young for a heart attack, so he passed the sensation off as a reaction from swallowing the pills too quickly.

He could only guess how many more of Darren's files had ended up on his desk without his knowledge. Mark made a mental note to cut down on his coffee consumption. Less time leaving his desk unattended meant less opportunity for the staff to sneak more work onto his desk.

He sighed and pushed aside the file he was working on that was already late. Tomorrow, Saturday, he would be back for another full day—and then some—likely again working until midnight. The building's night and weekend security staff almost knew him personally. In the past six months, he'd spent more time with the graveyard-shift night watchman than he had with his best friend.

"I need the file for a change of address, and then I'll give it right back." Joanne removed the file from his hand and returned to her desk.

With his hands once again empty, Mark stared at his computer. It had been left untouched for so long, the screen saver had come on, with varying actions of a pink rabbit toting a bass drum across the screen.

He let the rabbit continue to walk in circles across his monitor and stared blankly at the voluminous piles of client files around his office. Most of the files on his desk didn't need a CPA's handling. As the supervisor, he needed only to sign the files to verify that the calculations had been checked before turning the results over to the client. However, when each file took ten minutes, the accumulation of ten-minute intervals added up to hours. Days. Weeks.

Mark buried his face in his hands. The total had grown beyond what could be considered realistic for one person to do, yet he was trapped.

The phone rang, irritating the headache the painkillers hadn't yet had time to numb. In addition to the headache, his sore back, and his stiff shoulders, tightness enveloped his entire body.

He cleared his throat and tried his best to sound cheerful, when all he felt was exhaustion and defeat. "Mark Daniels. How can I help you?" As the words came out of his mouth, he regretted having to ask, because the question inevitably meant more work.

"Mark! It's Joe Dubois. How are you doing?"

"Fine," he said, first wondering if it were more appropriate to be polite than honest, then wondering why Joe was calling.

"I guess you've heard about your uncle Jack."

Something in his stomach went to war with the stale sandwich he'd eaten for lunch. The thing he regretted most about moving away from little Aidleyville to follow his career was missing his family and the friends with whom he'd grown up. After hearing bad news yesterday, he didn't think his uncle's business partner calling him at work during the day was a good sign. "Yes. Aunt Susan phoned me yesterday. Is Uncle Jack worse?"

"No, don't worry. He's showing improvement after the surgery. The reason I'm calling is that I need a favor, and it's a big one. Last night the compressor sprang a leak and hosed down the computer. I took it to the shop this morning, but the technician says the thing's fried. We've lost all the data, and that means all the restaurant's company records."

Mark released a sigh at learning his uncle wasn't worse, but his relief was short-lived. While computers made it easy for small businesses to do their own accounting, that unfortunately meant when things went wrong, they went very wrong.

Mark was afraid to know the answer, but he had to ask. "What about a backup?"

"The backups were all on the computer, so they're gone

with everything else. The last backup we have that wasn't on the computer is the one Jack gave our income tax accountant at our fiscal year end. Somehow, I've got to catch up on everything using all our paper invoices and what we've got on file here. I don't know how Jack does that stuff, and things are a real mess. I don't know if we even have everything we need. I at least need to somehow re-enter the bank balances, but I can't figure out Jack's system."

Joe stopped talking, but there was nothing Mark could say. He'd seen his uncle's system for handling the diner's business records. He had clients like his uncle. Many of their portfolios were now on his desk, driving him to an early grave.

After a lengthy silence, Joe resumed speaking. "I was wondering if you might come home for the weekend to help me. I'll pay for your flight." Joe's voice lowered to barely above a whisper. "I hate to ask, but we don't know who else to turn to."

The hum of the fluorescent lights and the far-off clicking of computer keys from the main office roared through Mark's head. The stacks of files on his desk suddenly seemed larger, hovering, threatening to envelop him with the problems and crises hidden within.

Surely, he could take a weekend off. He was at least entitled to weekends off. Technically.

He was now into the third year that he hadn't taken a vacation. They also owed him equivalent time off for the statutory holidays he'd worked, plus all the sick time he'd never taken or been paid for. For at least the past six months, he'd been working almost every weekend, plus he often stayed until midnight Monday to Friday during the week. He was entitled to a *lot* of time off, not just weekends. Probably months. Yet, whenever he wanted to stay home a day or two, he was, instead, reminded of another crushing deadline for another critical customer, obligating him to work yet more unpaid overtime. Sean, one of the company owners and his boss, always promised future benefits if he would work through another weekend. As of yet, not a single promise had been fulfilled.

Suddenly, more than anything he'd ever wanted before, Mark wanted to go home.

However, the responsibility for countless hours of uncompleted work lay heavily on his shoulders. To leave for the weekend only meant the backlogs would get worse instead of better. If he left for the weekend, he would suffer later, completely negating any good that one weekend away could accomplish.

But he really wanted to go home.

Desperate times call for desperate measures.

Mark bent over and reached into the wastepaper basket to pull out a crumpled faxed memo he'd received from the local career college. The administrator had requested businesses in the downtown area take a couple of students to work for free for a short period of time. In exchange, the businesses would provide the minimal training required to complete the practicum portion of the student's courses.

Keeping the phone cradled on his shoulder, Mark quickly smoothed out the wrinkles and skimmed over the memo, rereading the terms. At worst, surely two students could do in two weeks what he could accomplish in a weekend. At best, they could help the company catch up on at least some of the backlog.

If he worded himself carefully, he should be able to convince Sean that taking on two students for a practicum was not hiring them, because they weren't being paid in money. The only cost would be a little time from the current employees to guide the students. More work could ultimately be accomplished than the time lost in training them.

Such an arrangement would benefit all parties. The students would get the experience they needed to find a real job. S&B Accounting would have the extra help needed to get current in their customer files. Perhaps, seeing the difference a couple of bodies could make, with a little careful convincing, Mark could persuade Sean and Bob to hire one or even both of the students to keep it that way, despite the hiring ban.

The weight of the world lifted from his shoulders. The sun shone brighter. The birds on the ledge outside his window sang more sweetly.

Mark couldn't hold back his smile. "Sure, I'll help you. I could use a change of scenery. But I can certainly pay for my own flight. I'll even leave tonight."

"Great! I can hardly wait to see you! I'll tell your parents you're coming, although you're more than welcome to stay at our house. I've already checked with the airline. I might still get you booked on a cancellation that arrives tonight at seven-thirty. They'll e-mail you the flight confirmation. Just print it and present it at the ticket counter. And don't even think about paying for it. I'm booking, so I'm paying. No arguments. Being Friday and without your uncle here, I won't be able to get away from the diner and your parents have tickets for a play tonight. I'll send Chantelle to pick you up at the airport."

"Who? I don't know anyone named Chantelle. Why don't I just—"

Mark's words were interrupted by the sound of a resounding crash echoing over the phone line.

"I have to go. See you tonight. Chantelle, are you okay? Did the—"

A click sounded in Mark's ear, followed by a short silence, then the even buzz of the dial tone.

Mark hung up, still smiling. Not even the strange ending to the phone conversation could dampen Mark's spirit. He'd never done anything so impulsive in his life, but he didn't regret it. His weekends were his own, and he was well entitled to take them off, just like everyone else. And now, he could do it without guilt because he had plans to make everything better.

He had barely finished speaking to the college administrator when the E-mail arrived with his flight information.

Joanne returned with the McHenry file, handed it to him, and left without a word. Before opening the file, Mark phoned his parents and left a message on their answering machine that he was coming home for the weekend and he'd hook up with them at Joe's Diner after the theater performance.

He found himself humming as he completed the missing portion of Darren's calculations. After the weekend, he could face the rest of the files refreshed and ready, Darren would be back, and two students, eager to learn, would be waiting to perform.

Instead of picking up the next folder, and despite it not quite being the official end of the workday, Mark packed up his desk and shut down his computer.

He pushed his chair in with a flourish and left the building with a smile on his face.

He was going home.

If only he could remember someone named Chantelle.

two

Chantelle ran into the passenger pickup area just as the information board changed the status of Flight 736 from "in flight" to "arrived."

Before this afternoon, she'd never heard of Mark Daniels. She certainly didn't know what he looked like.

She didn't know what he was wearing, but Uncle Joe had given her a quick list of things to look for. Mark Daniels would be thin, fairly tall, with average brown hair. Uncle Joe couldn't remember Mark's eye color, but he thought they were brown. Mark was "a few" years older than Chantelle, but he didn't know how many. Mark also wore glasses as a child, but Uncle Joe couldn't remember Mark wearing them the last time they saw each other, so Uncle Joe concluded that Mark now wore contacts.

The only thing Uncle Joe was really positive about, which he had said with a wink and a nudge, was that Mark was fairly handsome. That one she didn't even want to consider. The last thing she needed was her uncle's matchmaking.

After all was said and done, the only thing she really knew about Mark was that he was traveling alone and had brown hair.

In desperation, despite her fears of appearing foolish, Chantelle frantically dug through her purse and pulled out the first piece of paper she could find. As the passengers began to approach the crowd of waiting people, she scribbled the name *Mark* on the back of the envelope for her phone bill and held it up for every lone man with any shade of brown hair, glasses or not.

Many of them smiled at her until they saw her sign with

another man's name on it.

One particularly handsome man wasn't swayed by the name on the envelope but winked as he passed. Chantelle was ready to throw the sign in the air and run away screaming. Just then, one "fairly handsome" brown-haired man without glasses and carrying a laptop computer case slowed so suddenly that the people behind him nearly bumped into him. He shuffled off to the side and stopped beside her.

He scanned her from head to toe, then one brown eyebrow rose. "Chantelle?"

"Mark Daniels?"

He smiled tightly and let out a nervous sigh. "Yes. I had no idea how I was going to recognize you. The sign was a good idea, although it's a little small." He paused while he eyed her up and down. "Now I know for sure that we really haven't met before."

Chantelle looked up at Mark as they moved away from the passing crowd. He was indeed tall, about six feet in height. His slightly shaggy hair was very average brown, as were his eyes, contrasting in every way with her own blond hair and blue eyes and her height of five-foot-three, in shoes. She pegged him to be in his early thirties, just as her uncle had said he would be. "You're not too skinny," Chantelle muttered.

"Pardon me?"

She could feel the heat of her blush in her cheeks. "Nothing. Uncle Joe told me approximately what you looked like. I was just comparing the list."

"At least you had a list. The only thing I knew about you was your first name." He looked pointedly down at her. She wondered if the top of her head could touch the bottom of his chin. Again, one eyebrow rose. "Should I know you?"

Chantelle shrugged her shoulders. "I don't know. Uncle Joe said you moved away not long after high school graduation, but we could have gone to school at the same time. We're supposedly only a few years apart in age. I'm twenty-nine, and I went to Central. How old are you?"

"I'm thirty-two. I went to Central, too. If you were a fresh-man when I was a senior, we probably wouldn't have noticed each other in such a big school. But I did get the school's math award and a scholarship. My picture is in the front hallway, along with all the other students who ever won anything in all the years of the school's existence. Although, at the time, I had a pair of real geeky glasses. After high school, I went to col-lege and worked in the kitchen at the diner for four years while I got my CPA, so you could have seen me then, although I don't remember you. I moved away to complete my full MBA and ended up getting a good job, so I never moved back to Aidleyville."

Chantelle narrowed her eyes to study him. She'd never been good at school and had graduated only by the mercy of her teachers. Mathematics was the only subject in which she hadn't required a tutor. Still, even having gone to the same high school, she didn't recognize him. She hadn't exactly hung out with the brainy kids, and she never looked at the school's award winners.

He jerked his head to the right. "Let's go get my suitcase and get out of here. I don't know if a two-hour time differ-ence and a two-and-a-half-hour flight is enough to bring about jet lag, but I'm definitely feeling something."

Chantelle blinked at his abrupt change of subject. "I was told to bring you back to the restaurant right away. Since it's Friday night and the weather is so warm, there are still lots of people having a late dinner. They're shorthanded without me."

He nodded and walked toward the baggage claim area so fast that Chantelle had to struggle to keep up with him. They squeezed into the crowd surrounding the luggage carousel, forcing them to stand so close they rubbed arms. Together they watched the first piece of luggage poke through the opening and slide down the chute.

"My suitcase is black with a strip of duct tape on the side."

Chantelle turned toward him, even though all his concentration was on the opening for the chute. "I can carry your laptop if that would make it easier to grab your suitcase when it comes by."

"That's a good idea."

He turned to surrender the black canvas case. As he did, Chantelle once again searched his face to see if she might recognize something familiar about him or imagine what he might have looked like in high school.

The second they made eye contact, Chantelle's breath caught. Glasses or not, if she'd ever met him before, she would have recognized him instantly. Not that he was movie-star handsome, but he wasn't bad, despite the dark circles under his eyes.

High cheekbones and a very straight nose matched a decisive jawline and a strong mouth. Without knowing him, one look would tell anyone in the vicinity that he meant what he said, and no one in their right mind would question him. Of course, his height helped that persona.

His commanding appearance aside, the thing that struck her the most was his eyes. Mark's brown eyes were the exact same shade as his hair, something she found strangely fascinating. He had a no-nonsense attitude and disposition; yet once she looked closely, the start of crow's-feet at the corners of his eyes changed his whole demeanor to one of kindness and a good heart, for anyone who dared to make direct eye contact—which she did. The contrast between his eyes and the rest of him intrigued her, making her want to know more about him.

The laptop no longer in his hands, Mark once again turned to the baggage chute. "Have you heard anything about my uncle? Last I heard he was doing well after surgery, but no one told me what kind of surgery."

"He had to have pins put in one leg, and he's got some internal injuries. But I heard he's doing okay. Considering."

Mark nodded, still not once letting his attention to the baggage chute lapse. "You said you're working for the diner. Years ago when I worked there, everyone was either a relative of mine or Joe's or went to their church."

Chantelle nodded. "Nothing has changed. When he's short-handed at the restaurant, Uncle Joe always manages to find someone from one family or the other. This time, that person was me."

"So you haven't been working for your uncle very long, then?"

Chantelle shook her head. While Mark continued to watch the suitcases come through the opening, she continued to watch him. "Counting today, two days."

"There's my suitcase." They waited in silence until the bag dropped down and made its way round to them. Mark reached over and pulled it from the carousel in one fluid motion, then stepped back. "This is all I have. We can go now."

Chantelle hurried him as fast as she could through the building. To her relief, her car was exactly as she had left it, in the ten-minute parking section—slightly crooked, but still where it was supposed to be, even though she'd been longer than ten minutes.

"I was really surprised when Joe called me. Things must be pretty bad."

"They are. Uncle Joe doesn't like the computer much. He especially didn't have anything nice to say when he took it to the shop and they told him it was hopeless. I know he could learn, but he's afraid to do anything but the basic daily deposit and a little bit of E-mail. He asked me if I could do anything with the paperwork. I could probably enter most of it once I figured out what I was doing, but I wouldn't be able to do anything more than basic data entry. That's why he called you."

"Well, he's got me, at least for most of the weekend. Do you know if Uncle Jack is allowed visitors beyond immediate family yet? I'd sure like to see him."

"I don't know. They allowed Uncle Joe to see him, but only once and for only five minutes. I think they didn't want to worry you. He's still listed as serious."

Mark's face turned to stone. He said nothing on the short trip back to the restaurant, and Chantelle didn't push it. As much as she wanted to tell him everything would be all right, she didn't know for sure, so she left him alone with his thoughts.

❧

Chantelle led Mark through the front door of Joe's Diner, where Uncle Joe was busy as usual, seating customers and working the cash register. As soon as he saw Mark, laptop in hand, Uncle Joe stepped out from behind the counter. He grasped Mark's free hand in a firm handshake and rested his other hand on Mark's opposite shoulder.

"Thanks for coming. You have no idea how much this means to me. It's great to see you after all these years. You're looking good. A little thin, but good."

For the first time since she'd met him, Mark really smiled. It was a beautiful smile, and the little crow's feet crinkled at the corners of his eyes.

Mark pointedly looked down to her uncle's waistline, or lack thereof. "And you still have a little too much around the middle."

To see if she could make him smile again, Chantelle started to extend her arm to pat her uncle's rounded tummy. As she did so, Kevin called out from the kitchen. "Chantelle, you're back! Three-oh and three-one!"

She drew her hand back. "Excuse me. He's calling that my orders are up for a couple of my tables. I'll leave you two alone."

As she walked away, she heard Mark speak to her uncle with a lowered voice. "I don't remember it being so busy in here at this hour on a Friday night."

"I've never seen it like this before. Five minutes after Chantelle left, an entire softball team came in, and every one of them ordered a meal. Ten minutes before you came in, another group of about twenty people came in." His voice lowered even more. "I think they all know Chantelle. She's been really great for business, and it's only been two days."

Chantelle collected a tray of dinners and proceeded to deliver them to the first large group, which was a mixed soft-ball team she belonged to a couple of years ago. When she wanted to quit, they'd all tried to convince her to stay. However, after a few incidents with the bat, combined with her total inability to aim the ball properly, she decided to quit before she hurt someone other than herself. Her short membership cured her desire to participate in organized sports, but she often went to the games to cheer her friends on from the safety of the bleachers.

Her path to deliver their orders took her close enough to the reception area to hear Mark and her uncle's continuing conversation.

Mark didn't see her as he spoke. "If she's serving, how come she's not wearing a uniform?"

Uncle Joe lowered his head to respond, but Chantelle heard him anyway. "Both uniforms that fit her are in the laundry. At lunch time she spilled coffee down the front of herself, and then she had a slight accident with a couple of children who shouldn't have been running down the aisle."

Chantelle gritted her teeth. Her first day in the kitchen, those things had been her fault. After her little accident with the sugar, it was no surprise when Uncle Joe moved her out of the kitchen and into serving so quickly. She'd been totally devoid of experience. Timing the orders so that every item on the plate was ready at the same time was nearly impossible. Organizing all the orders for the same group to be delivered together was even worse. Knowing now what she didn't know then, she couldn't imagine keeping it up all day long, day after day.

But now she was officially a server and no longer confined

to a cramped work area. This time, neither incident had been her fault.

"Chantelle! Three-two and three-four!"

She hurried back to serve the next couple of tables, telling herself that she didn't have to care what Mark thought. In a couple of days, he would be gone and she probably would never see him again. His opinion shouldn't have mattered. Yet it did.

Chantelle returned to the kitchen for the coffeepot. Out of the corner of her eye, she watched Uncle Joe and Mark. They appeared to be studying Brittany as she took new orders from the other large group, which was the College-and-Careers group from her church.

Uncle Joe checked his watch. "Mark, would you mind helping in the kitchen? I think Kevin and Evelyn are going to need it."

"Of course."

"Chantelle! Three-three and three-five!"

Chantelle hurried to deliver the orders while Mark disappeared into the kitchen. As she slid the plates onto a tray, she heard him introducing himself to Kevin and Evelyn.

"Yes, we heard you were going to help out," Evelyn murmured. Through the serving window, Chantelle saw Evelyn rip the corners of the bills to indicate that orders had been filled; then she slid the plates on the counter for Brittany to deliver. "Will you really be able to fix everything?"

"I hope so. Maybe not all this weekend, but I at least should be able to get it to a point where Joe can enter what's current."

Since Brittany was still busy, Chantelle delivered the orders. When she returned for the coffeepot, she couldn't help but hear the continuing conversation from within the kitchen.

"Wow, that's so interesting! Your job must be fascinating!"

Chantelle watched as Mark heaped a serving of fries and a scoop of coleslaw onto each plate while Evelyn dressed the buns for the burgers.

"Not really," Mark mumbled back. "Sometimes I wish I had never taken that job."

Chantelle gritted her teeth. She couldn't believe he wouldn't be grateful for a high-paying, titled management job that came with a private office. Right now, Chantelle would have taken any position offered to her, office or not. She had proven her desperation by the fact that she now worked at near-minimum wage in a job for which she wasn't suited.

Mark picked up two of the plates. "Chantelle!" he called out, then began to turn around. "Two-sev—" His voice lowered in volume and faded into silence. "Sorry. I didn't know you were there. Table two-seven." He slid the plates onto the counter, ripped the corner of the bill, and tucked it under one of the plates.

"That's okay," she mumbled as she checked the plates against the order, then slipped the paper into her apron pocket. "I didn't mean to listen in to your conversation with Evelyn."

"It's okay. I know there isn't much privacy in this busy kitchen. I shouldn't complain about my job. Really, every job is what you make it."

"I guess," she muttered, turned around, and pasted on a smile as she delivered the orders to her friends at table twenty-seven.

If every job was what a person made it, Uncle Joe should have fired her hours ago for making the serving job a nuclear disaster.

Even though today it hadn't been her fault, nothing had gone much differently than her day in the kitchen. During the lunch period, someone bumped her and an entire cup of coffee spilled down her front when it toppled off the tray. Fortunately, Uncle Joe and everyone else had been more worried about burns to her skin and had not paid attention to the mess. In this case, the coffee had been cold, left by a customer who'd taken one too many refills.

Then at suppertime, the mothers of a couple of preschoolers hadn't been watching their children and allowed them to climb in and out of the chairs unattended instead of demanding the children stay seated. The children had run right in front of her when she was on her way to a table in the far corner of her area. Unable to see them beneath the large tray as she walked, she'd tripped on them, spilling everything she carried, then she'd landed on top of the mess. That little accident had broken three plates and two cups, in addition to sending fries flying onto three nearby tables, to say nothing of the splatted food on the carpet and her uniform.

Good fortune was on her side. Everyone in the area had seen that it wasn't her fault and that the situation could have been much worse. No one had been injured by flying objects, and Uncle Joe said the carpet needed a steam cleaning anyway.

Those incidents had been enough to remove waitressing from Chantelle's list of potential future jobs. Fearing that things would get worse before they got better, Chantelle had offered to quit as soon as Uncle Joe found someone to replace her. He refused to talk about it.

She spent the rest of the evening in a daze, trying not to think of what disasters would await her tomorrow—Saturday—the restaurant's busiest day.

three

Mark sipped his coffee and sighed while he waited for his laptop computer to boot up. He hadn't had time to install the accounting program last night, but that hadn't been a bad thing. Doing something that didn't involve his computer had been a welcome change, even though he hadn't come all this way to work in Uncle Jack's kitchen. As tired as he had been, it had also been good to stand while he worked instead of sitting behind a desk, his only movement being his fingers as he typed.

Of course, all thoughts of work in any form disappeared when his parents arrived to pick him up. The last time he'd seen them had been over three years ago, his last vacation. The sniffles his mother tried her best to hide only told him that it had been far too long and that he would have to come home more often.

Now, after a good night's sleep, Mark was ready to face the day. His parents had loaned him their car so he could drive to the hospital later in the afternoon to see Uncle Jack. Since he wasn't immediate family, an exception has been made to allow Mark to see his uncle for five minutes, but only because of his uncle's insistence. Until then, he had work to do. Nice as it was to take a trip down memory lane, it was even better to be doing what he did best, which was to sort and enter all the business's financial transactions.

Over the next two days, Mark planned to properly input all the invoices, purchases, payroll, taxes, and other expenses, then reconcile everything against the daily sales and deposits, cash flow and bank statements, to thereby produce a workable and manageable database.

He knew he wouldn't be able to do everything in just one

weekend. Therefore, he planned to finish it up at home, where he could also work up the monthly profit-and-loss statements for the past year. After that, he would compile statistics to predict peak periods to help his uncle and Joe better structure their staffing, which was the biggest expense.

Two tiny raps sounded on the office door. It opened before he replied.

Chantelle peeked her head in. "Feeling a bit more chipper this morning? Can I warm up your coffee?"

He smiled. "Yes, thanks."

Chantelle entered the room. She wore a fresh, clean uniform, smartly displaying Joe's Diner's navy, yellow, and white logo colors, the way she should have been last night. Working in the kitchen, he wasn't required to wear a uniform, but both Joe and Uncle Jack had always been very particular about the servers' dress code. Inwardly, he winced at Chantelle's pink sneakers, but he trusted that she would rectify that situation within a week.

She poured his coffee, left a small handful of cream containers on the table, and disappeared, leaving the door open behind her.

Mark shook his head while he waited for the program to install. He'd already seen the breakage report for the last two days, higher than usual, most of it attributable to Chantelle. As well as the expense of the dishes and wasted food, someone would have to steam-clean the carpet, a situation also attributable to Chantelle. However, he'd also seen the notes Joe had made. They had witnesses who saw two children dart in front of her and trip her. Fortunately, no one had been hurt, so they weren't going to face any lawsuits for injury or trauma to the children.

On the bright side, Chantelle had come on short notice when asked. When she wasn't having some kind of accident, she worked hard and cheerfully, so Mark had to give her credit for that.

Since none of the customers could see inside the office, Mark didn't bother to get up to close the door. Just as he had last night, he found the familiar background noise of the restaurant comforting, especially compared to the sterile atmosphere of his office back in the city. Here, the customers were happy, the servers cheerful, and all the staff worked together without bickering. Every once in awhile he could hear Joe's boisterous and welcome laugh when another regular customer entered. He also heard Chantelle talking with customers far more than anyone else who worked there.

He didn't put in his own order for lunch until the rush was over. Just as in years gone by, the kitchen staff would pile his plate with extra fries and a double scoop of the diner's famous coleslaw, and he would get his food order for free because, for the weekend, he was considered staff.

"Mark! Chantelle! Order up!" a part-timer called out from the kitchen.

Two identical plates sat on the pickup counter when he answered the call.

Chantelle reached out toward one of the plates, then froze with her hand in midair. She glanced back and forth between the two identical orders.

Mark stood beside her. "Mushroom burger and fries?"

"Yes, but I ordered mine with cheese. If we're both having lunch at the same time, why don't you join me in the staff room?"

Mark had planned on eating his lunch while he worked, but Chantelle's invitation reminded him that he promised himself he was never again going to work through his breaks. Just because he was working at his uncle's restaurant for the weekend, and doing it as a favor, didn't negate the fact that he was still working.

"That sounds like a good idea."

They each picked up one plate, helped themselves to a drink, and walked toward the staff room in the rear of the building.

"Who was that in the kitchen today?" Mark asked over his shoulder as they walked. "I met Evelyn last night, but short of looking up the staff schedule, I don't know anyone here except Brittany. And you, of course."

"That's Jorge. He only works every second Saturday. He has another job, so Jorge and his wife trade which Saturdays they work so one of them can stay home with their kids."

"That's a rather unique arrangement."

Chantelle shrugged her shoulders as they entered the small staff room. She set her meal and drink on the table. "They need the money, but it's too much for Jorge to work six days a week, every week. The same with Helena. That's his wife's name, by the way. So, that's the arrangement Uncle Joe made. The only reason I know is because Uncle Joe had to check the schedule last night to see what hours he wanted me to work today, and he explained it to me. He said my start time would depend on who else was working. I got the early shift, as you can see."

They both peeked under the buns as soon as they sat, then traded plates without a word.

Chantelle folded her hands on the table in front of her. "Can we pause for a word of thanks before we eat?"

"Sure." Mark also clasped his hands, then bowed his head. He knew she was waiting for him to speak, but he remained silent. After a few seconds, she said a short prayer over their food, including asking for a blessing over the day in general at the restaurant. She ended with an enthusiastic "amen." Mark responded with significantly less emphasis and reached for the bottle of ketchup.

Mark didn't plan to talk. All he wanted was to eat quickly and return to his computer, but Chantelle didn't seem to be in any hurry. While he squeezed a blob of ketchup onto his plate, Chantelle folded her hands in front of her and watched him while she talked. "The staffing schedule is going to be changed today because Uncle Joe didn't have time to do it

Thursday or Friday with so much happening. With your uncle off, Uncle Joe first put me in the kitchen, but he changed his mind."

Mark slid the bottle toward her and shuffled the overflowing burger in his hands to get a good grip on it, readying it to take his first bite. Chantelle grasped the ketchup bottle, but instead of helping herself, she pushed it aside. She leaned toward him across the table, then quickly looked from side to side as if she were about to share a profound secret.

Mark opened his mouth, about to take his first bite. At the touch of Chantelle's fingertips on his arm, he froze, the burger in front of him, his mouth gaping. Making eye contact over the top of the dripping burger, he couldn't move in any way, not even to put the burger down. Just like a moth caught in the deadly pull of a flame, all he could do was stare back at her, completely transfixed.

Her big, blue eyes widened. He'd never seen eyes so blue. At the airport, all he'd noticed was her slightly crooked nose. Now, looking at her face-to-face, he wondered why he hadn't noticed. Not that she was drop-dead gorgeous, but she certainly wasn't bad.

A mane of unruly hair so blond it was almost white framed a dainty face, highlighting a cute pixie chin. A series of multicolored hair clips that probably were meant to be in a straight line, none of which matched the uniform, barely managed to keep the mass of curls under some semblance of control. It shouldn't have surprised him. From what he'd seen and heard so far, Chantelle Dubois was as wild and out of control as her hair. Even while they were sitting still, allegedly just to eat and talk, after being on her feet all morning long, one foot tapped constantly against her chair.

The woman radiated boundless, unchecked energy, which made him feel even more tired than he really was. If he were smart, he would excuse himself and run back to the office, but he couldn't force himself to move. He could only lower the burger to the plate and watch her as she spoke.

"Things weren't working out for me in the kitchen," she said in an exaggerated whisper, then straightened and cleared her throat. "Uncle Joe moved Evelyn into the kitchen while Jack's gone. Now he has to rearrange the schedule a little because he doesn't want me working with only part-timers. He said that's because I've never done this before."

After seeing what had happened outside of the kitchen, Mark could only guess at what happened inside the kitchen to make Joe pull Chantelle out after only one day on the job. He quickly lifted the burger and took a bite. Then he grunted a response that she could have interpreted any way she pleased, sparing him from having to reply.

Chantelle finally bit into her burger. "Are you really going to be able to fix up all that stuff Jack left?" she mumbled around the food in her mouth before she swallowed in one, noisy gulp. "When Uncle Joe saw all the diner's paperwork for the last two years just stuffed into boxes, I thought he was going to faint."

Mark dabbed his mouth with the corner of his napkin, then pushed the extra napkin he'd brought across the table toward Chantelle. "I'll get it all entered one way or another. I can't tell yet if anything is missing. I might have to take home everything I don't get done once I've sorted what goes with the current fiscal year. I know I'm not going to get everything reconciled before I leave tomorrow. It's pretty disorganized. And that's being nice."

"Does that mean you'll be coming back next weekend?"

Mark nearly told her that since he'd taken this weekend off, he'd have to work doubly hard next weekend and for many weeks to come. But the words wouldn't come.

During the cab ride to the airport yesterday, doubts had begun to assail him, making him question his decision to leave town for the weekend. It had been too late to change his mind.

Once the plane was airborne, Mark didn't even turn on his laptop. He was simply too tired. All he could do was close his eyes for the duration of the flight. However, between the worry and drinking so much coffee all day long, Mark found himself too wired to sleep. But it didn't matter. In his rush to leave, he hadn't uploaded any files to work on. He hadn't even taken a book to occupy his time during the flight. He didn't have the energy to strike up a conversation with the man sitting next to him. All he could do was sit in his self-imposed darkness and think.

He'd ended up thinking about work. Lately all he did, besides driving to and from work and sleeping to get enough rest to go back to work, was work. Since he'd been awarded the management position, he'd been so busy that his only break was going to church on Sunday mornings. Except, for the last year or so, he hadn't been going every Sunday. In fact, he couldn't remember the last time he'd been to church at all, much less what the message had been.

At first, he felt guilty. However, after awhile he found that not going to church didn't make a difference in his life. With his ever-increasing workload, he found himself catching up on some much-needed sleep on Sunday mornings. Then, when he awoke, instead of going to the late service, he went to the office.

Not long after being promoted to his supervisory position, the people whom he thought were his friends at work stopped inviting him to their social outings. He never saw his friends from his last year of college anymore; they were all too busy as well. Since he stopped going to church, he seldom saw that circle of friends, either. He hadn't been out on a date for ages, nor any other social outing that did not involve a business function.

Alone on the plane, with only his thoughts for company, Mark did something he hadn't done for a long time. He talked to God, even though Mark felt God never listened to him. He told God he was tired of the rat race. Tired of running around in circles. Tired of living only to work for a company where no one appreciated him. The more he did, the more they expected him to do.

He didn't receive any answers. He hadn't expected to.

Slowly his thoughts drifted back to where he was—sitting in the small lunchroom, across the table from Chantelle, who was sitting, watching him, waiting for him to say something.

Mark felt his ears heat up. "I'm sorry. I didn't mean to be rude. What were you saying? I got lost thinking about something else."

"That's okay. Don't worry about it. I was wondering if you were going to come to church with us tomorrow."

Mark gulped, wondering if she'd been able to read his mind. "Church?"

"Yes. Normally I go to my own church, but Uncle Joe asked everyone to go to his church so we can all have lunch at their house after. Your aunt Susan is going to be there, and so are your parents. He's also invited me to go with him on Wednesday, when they have a special Bible study night. Uncle Joe says it's really special, almost like a mini church service. They have a worship time with music, and it's really informal. Apparently, lots of people go there who aren't comfortable in the more formal setting Sunday morning. I usually go to weekly Bible studies, but they're in someone's home. I've never been to a service on a weeknight, informal or not."

"Church service on Wednesday night?" As if he should be concerned about a midweek church service. It had been a long, long time since he'd attended any church function, Sunday or otherwise.

All seriousness left Chantelle's face as she started to smile, her grin growing, almost in slow motion. Her eyes sparkled, and she looked so happy she practically glowed. She took on such an angelic look, it started to make Mark nervous.

"Uncle Joe says that due to this Wednesday night ministry,

some of the people who won't go to church on Sundays but will go on Wednesdays have made decisions to become Christians. Isn't that wonderful?"

Mark bowed his head and concentrated on swirling a fry into the blob of ketchup on his plate. "Yeah," he muttered. "That's great."

They sat in silence for awhile, each of them simply eating, until Chantelle finished her burger and about half her fries.

"You know, I think I've done all the talking. Tell me about yourself. What it's like to move away from where you were born and raised? Are you going out with your parents tonight? Somewhere special since you haven't been home for awhile? Or are you just going to stay home and relax? I guess you're going to see your uncle in the hospital later, aren't you?"

Mark raised his head and stared into Chantelle's wide, expectant eyes. When he didn't speak immediately, her eyes widened even more.

"I don't know which question to answer first," he mumbled.

"Uncle Joe says you're an accountant and that you work in a big high-rise office tower in the middle of downtown. Why don't you start by telling me about your job? All I've ever done is data entry and ordinary office jobs. What's it like to be a manager and have your own office?"

Evelyn had asked him about his job yesterday. For the first time in his life, he'd acted on a whim and left his job and responsibilities behind. Even though he had second thoughts once he boarded the plane, it had felt unbelievably good to get up and walk away. Whether or not it was worth it, he would decide later.

"It's a job. A lot of pressure, a lot of stress. I'm finally away from the office, and I want to keep it that way."

"Oh. . ." Chantelle's voice trailed off, she bowed her head, and dipped one of the fries into her blob of ketchup. "Sorry," she muttered. "I won't mention it again."

If Mark hadn't felt bad enough before, he felt even worse

now. "That's okay," he murmured. "I didn't realize until now it was such a sore spot. Don't worry about it. I'm also a little tired. Taking into account the time difference, my body-clock tells me I got up at four-thirty A.M."

The reappearance of Chantelle's smile told Mark she forgave him for his surly behavior.

"That's almost inhuman, isn't it? Yesterday I worked the late shift, but today I was assigned the early one. I had to get up at five-thirty to be here, ready to start at six-thirty when the diner opens. Even with my other job, I never had to get up so early. I don't know how people do it."

"It's not that bad. I get up at six for work every day. That's only a half-hour difference."

Chantelle gave an exaggerated shudder and squeezed her eyes shut for a second. "Maybe I'm just feeling sorry for myself because I have to go to bed at nine-thirty. That's so early; but if I don't get eight hours of sleep, I can be a real bear."

In his entire life, he couldn't remember meeting anyone more cheerful and bubbly than Chantelle. It was almost irritating, except he couldn't be angry with anyone so consistently happy. He couldn't imagine Chantelle being a bear under any circumstances.

He started to tell her that he never got more than six hours' sleep a night, more usually five, and that he did fine, but he stopped himself. For the first time, Mark began to wonder if lack of sleep might have something to do with the dragged-out feeling he'd been living with for the past couple of years.

At first, he got away with working the occasional evening until midnight, making the long drive home, and still getting up at six. But, as time went on, he found himself working late more and more often. Without realizing it, his ever-increasing late hours caught up with him. In addition to the lack of sleep, the stress and responsibility was taking its toll on him, both mentally and physically. The only times he got enough sleep were on the weekends. Then he didn't have to get up as early to go to work, even though he still went, supposedly on his own time. He only wished he could do something about it. Taking the practicum students from the business college was a good first step. Although, Monday, he would face his boss's reaction to what he'd done without first going through proper channels for authorization.

As soon as Chantelle popped the last fry into her mouth, she stood. "That half-hour sure went fast. I have to get back to work. If I don't get a chance to talk to you before then, I'll see you at church tomorrow morning. Bye."

Before he could think of a response, Chantelle disappeared.

Mark began to wonder if she was always so abrupt or if she knew he would try to come up with some excuse not to go. On the other hand, after his long talk with God on the plane, he wondered if he shouldn't at least give church a try.

Since he suspected that nothing would change for awhile once he returned home, Mark shrugged it off, telling himself that, if nothing else, going to church was good for him.

As soon as he finished the last of his fries, Mark picked up both plates and both glasses, walked into the kitchen, and placed them in the dishwasher rack. While he was there, he peeked over the pickup counter and into the restaurant and watched Chantelle. While she wrote an order on the notepad, the tip of her tongue peeked out of the corner of her mouth. Quite frankly, he couldn't see what on the menu could possibly require as much concentration as she took to jot down the variations of the lunchtime hamburger menu.

He continued to stand in one spot, watching as she moved on to the second woman in the party of four and took her order with the same painstaking care. When she moved on to the first man, however, she didn't write anything down. She stood in one spot while he talked, listening intently. Instead of writing anything down, she held her finger up in the air and glanced toward the kitchen, then started walking toward the small opening joining the kitchen with the restaurant.

Upon her arrival, she rested her palms on the edge of the counter and leaned in. Mark had no doubt that she was also up on her tiptoes.

"One of the customers is asking if we can put some grated cheese on the breadsticks and broil it until it's melted and slightly golden. He said they once did it for him at Lizziano's down the street, but his wife wanted to come here. I didn't know what to say."

Jorge narrowed one eye, turned his head toward the oven, and then turned back to Chantelle. "I see no reason why not."

"Will there be an extra charge for that?"

"I don't know. You'd have to ask Joe."

"Okay. Thanks."

In a flash, she turned to the table, signaled an *okay* sign in the air, then hurried to the front counter, where she repeated the same request to Uncle Joe. When he shook his head, Chantelle turned once more to the table in question, clenched her fist in the air, and pulled it down in a gesture of triumph, then returned to the table, practically skipping.

Mark couldn't believe her theatrics.

"I guess that meant 'no extra charge' then," Jorge said, smiling.

Mark crossed his arms over his chest. "Looks like it," he said, not smiling.

"I know what you're thinking. I've been watching her all day. She's like that to everybody."

"I don't know if I should be surprised."

"I hear she's another relative."

Mark didn't know if he should have confessed that he, too, was a relative, so he simply nodded.

"Speaking of relatives, I hear you're Jack's nephew, here to fix things up after that accident with the computer. No secrets around here. It's a great place to work. Jack and Joe are great guys."

"I know. I used to work here when I was in college. Not

much has changed. Not even the decorating, although it looks like they got all the chairs recovered."

"Jack likes consistency, that's for sure. Here comes Chantelle with that order for the breadstick table. Just wait until you see her orders. She always makes sure to write out every detail in longhand. We never have any doubt about what her tables want. She even makes notes about who gets what."

Mark couldn't decide if that was good or bad. When he was in the kitchen, the servers and the cooks always knew all the abbreviations and shortcuts, and he'd never seen a server write down which order belonged to which person. He suspected that no one had yet found the time to teach her the codes or what was necessary versus not necessary. He thought he might do Joe a favor and teach them to her, except he was here for more valuable work than teaching a server that *N O* simply meant "no onions."

"Excuse me. I should be back in the office. It was nice meeting you, Jorge."

He didn't see Chantelle for the rest of the afternoon, although he heard her voice on a regular basis through the open doorway. He could certainly tell when she left, because not only did most of the current staff wish her a pleasant evening as she walked out the main door, some of the customers did, too.

Mark shook his head as he tried once more to make sense of the jumble of his uncle's disorganized paperwork. In the back of his mind, he realized that just as he'd heard some of the staff say they would miss Chantelle for the rest of the workday, he would miss her, too. Not because she actually talked to him or had anything to do with him, except for their short lunch break together. Listening to her exploits as she went about her day serving, Chantelle proved to be very entertaining. From a distance.

He gritted his teeth as he once more came upon the shrinkage report from the day before.

One of the reasons he found Chantelle so entertaining

today stemmed from her absence of broken dishes and spilled drinks, unlike the other days since he'd arrived. Since tomorrow was Sunday, instead of seeing her at the diner, he would be seeing her at church.

At that thought, Mark's hands froze over the keyboard. If she behaved the same way at church that she did at work, he didn't know if he wanted to see her out in public. However, for some reason, it was important to Joe that they all attend church together. Joe had become like a second father to him when he worked for the diner during his college days. For that reason, as well as being his favorite uncle's best friend, he would go.

four

The pastor raised his hands, tilted his head back, and closed his eyes. "Go!" he called out. "And may the peace of Christ be with you always!"

"A-MEN!" the congregation chorused.

Immediately, the instruments began to play. At the same time, the worship team hummed the melody of the last song in perfect four-part harmony. The lights in the seating area brightened, while the lights at the front dimmed. Most of the congregation began to file out of the sanctuary, but a few people remained kneeling at the front, tears streaming down their faces, while the elders prayed with them. The difference in the lighting created an unseen line not to cross, unless a person had a prayer to bring to the altar, giving those at the front their privacy.

Chantelle felt on the verge of tears, herself. "Wow," she muttered, both to clear her throat and give herself some time to get a grip. "I've never been to a service like this in my life. What about you?"

Mark's voice beside her came out strangely choked as well. "No. Never."

She stuffed her bulletin, all scrunched up and scribbled full of notes, into her purse. "This has given me a lot to think about. I think I have a lot of reading to do. I wonder if I can get a tape?"

Uncle Joe and Aunt Ellen smiled at each other, then turned to face her.

"Yes, you can," Aunt Ellen said. "They make tapes to give away to those who were unable to attend. I'm sure they'll give one to a guest who wants to hear Pastor's sermon again."

On their way out, many people stopped to speak to Susan, asking questions and expressing their concern for Jack. Most offered to bring her food, to give her more time to spend at the hospital, which Chantelle thought was very nice.

"Is everyone hungry?" Aunt Ellen asked as their large group finally made it to the door. "I think we all see too much of that diner, so everyone is invited over to our house for lunch. I made a big casserole yesterday. It's been warming in the oven while we've been gone, just waiting for us to get home and eat."

Chantelle wondered exactly how large the casserole in question would be. Not only was Susan coming, but they'd also invited their daughter Marella, along with Marella's husband and their son, Bradley. Adding Mark's parents, Hank and Leslie, and of course Mark and herself, the total came to ten people. She also wondered how they were going to fit everyone in her aunt's small kitchen.

Lunch turned out to be a crowded but friendly affair. She'd never met Hank and Leslie before, but they were so warm and open that, within an hour, she felt like she'd known them for years. They talked so much, enjoying each other's company, that in order to make Mark's flight time, Aunt Ellen brought a box of hamburgers out of the freezer and insisted everyone stay.

The entire time Uncle Joe barbecued, he complained, in fun, that because he saw far too many hamburgers at the diner, he didn't want to see them at home, too. His playful protests made Chantelle suspect that she would soon feel the same way about eating restaurant meals, although she couldn't compare the store-bought oven fries to the *real* fries the restaurant made in the deep fryer.

The last hamburger had barely disappeared off the plate when Uncle Joe looked at the time. "Mark, you should collect your suitcase and we should get going. You don't want to miss your flight."

Mark nodded. "The weekend sure went fast. I didn't get as much done as I'd hoped."

Uncle Joe patted him on the shoulder. "That's okay. I certainly appreciate everything you did. What I needed most was to be able to enter the day-to-day deposits and purchases, and you've done much more than that."

"If you don't mind, I'd like to take some of it home and keep working on it. I can always e-mail the data file and courier the receipts back." He stopped and broke out into a big grin, once again making Chantelle think it was a shame he didn't smile more often. "Or I can make a point of coming home more often and bring everything with me then." He paused to look at his mother. "I promise it won't be so long next time. I've had a wonderful time. I didn't realize how much I needed this. But it is time for me to go home."

Chantelle set her mug down on the coffee table and turned to Mark. "Do you know that you just called both places home? That must be so strange."

He shrugged his shoulders, but didn't reply.

Chantelle wondered what his life in the big city must be like, to have such a busy and active social life that he was never home. Unlike Mark, Chantelle spent most of her time at her apartment, more so lately because, until two days ago, she didn't have a job to go to during the daytime, which also meant that she could no longer afford to go out during the evenings.

Susan sighed. "This weekend has been much too short. I hardly got to see you. You spent most of your time at the diner, and I spent most of my time at the hospital."

Mark stood as well. "I know, but it couldn't be helped. The time went much too quickly." He checked his wristwatch. "Speaking of time, I had better get moving. I have to pick up my suitcase from Mom and Dad's, then stop by the diner to get that box of paperwork and my laptop on the way to the airport."

Uncle Joe stood next. "I don't know how I can ever thank you enough for coming. Ellen and I would like to see you off, too. We can go to the diner for you and then meet you at the airport. That will save you a bit of time since we're running a little late already. Hank, Leslie, I guess you're taking Mark to the airport?"

Hank nodded. "Yes."

"Susan?"

Susan turned to Mark. "If you don't mind, I'm going to go back to the hospital and see Jack, since I haven't seen him yet today. Thanks for coming, Mark, and have a good flight home."

"I will. Thanks."

Uncle Joe turned to Chantelle. "What about you? You can either come to the airport with us or someone can take you home."

Chantelle checked her watch, now sorry she'd accepted her uncle's offer to pick her up for church. Marella needed to take her son home to bed, not spending her time driving across town. Susan was obviously in a rush to get to the hospital to see her husband, so she didn't want to impose there, either. "I'd like to see Mark off, too."

At her words, Mark's eyebrows rose, and she thought that maybe his cheeks might have darkened a bit. She didn't want to give him any wrong ideas, but she didn't want him to feel insulted that the only reason she was going was because she didn't have a ride home.

Uncle Joe and Aunt Ellen gave Bradley a big hug and kiss, along with promises to take him out next weekend, and everyone went their separate ways.

Because they had to go to the diner first, which was in the opposite direction as the airport, Chantelle could tell Uncle Joe was rushing far too much. She didn't have to check the speedometer to know he was speeding. Before she knew it, they were at the diner. She ran in with Uncle Joe for the laptop and the huge box of receipts. In far less time than it had ever taken her to drive it, they were at the airport. Chantelle thought it only by good fortune that Uncle Joe made it without a ticket.

Chantelle carried the laptop and Uncle Joe carried the box as they hurried into the main terminal, catching up to Mark just as he was collecting his boarding pass. "Here's your laptop. I guess you'll want to check this box."

"Yes. They now have restrictions as to how much you can carry on. I'm certainly not checking my laptop."

Uncle Joe thunked the heavy box onto the scale. The clerk tagged it and sent it on its way down the conveyor belt.

"You can go to the boarding area now. They'll be calling for final boarding for your flight in about half an hour. Have a pleasant flight, and thank you for flying with us."

Mark tucked the boarding pass into his shirt pocket. "Let's go have a coffee. We'll just have to listen carefully for the last boarding call and keep an eye on the time so I can run in at the last minute."

When everyone stepped toward the cafeteria, Chantelle turned around to ask if anyone knew the way to the ladies' room. At the same time she opened her mouth to speak, Uncle Joe's footsteps faltered. He reached out and touched Aunt Ellen's arm, causing her to stop as well.

"It's so hot in here," he mumbled, swiping at his brow with his forearm.

Chantelle glanced to the windows and the warm sunshine outside. The afternoon had been hot, but it was now after six and not as stifling as it had been earlier. Inside, the airport's air-conditioning made it much cooler than outside. And for a man who thought it was hot, Uncle Joe's face was alarmingly pale.

Chantelle stopped walking and faced her uncle. "Uncle Joe? Are you okay?"

Everyone in their group slowly shuffled to a halt and also turned when Uncle Joe stopped walking.

"I'm fine," he said, but his voice came out strained. "Maybe I need to sit dow—"

His voice trailed off as his face paled even more. Both eyes widened, his mouth opened, and he pressed both hands to his chest. Instead of gasping for air, Uncle Joe stiffened, then crumpled to the floor, knocking down a number of the chrome posts as he fell.

Mark thrust his laptop at Chantelle, letting go before she had a chance to grab it properly. While she stood in one spot fumbling with Mark's laptop, Mark ran to her uncle and dropped to the ground on his hands and knees.

"Joe!" he called out as he pressed his fingers into his throat. "Can you respond? Say something!"

He waited for only two seconds, but they were the longest two seconds of Chantelle's life.

Uncle Joe didn't move. He'd paled even more; his skin was a ghastly shade of pale gray.

Mark lifted his head. "Call 9-1-1 and page a doctor!" he called out to the woman at the check-in counter. "I think he's having a heart attack!"

Chantelle watched as time moved in slow motion. She forced herself to breathe as she stood, her feet frozen to the floor.

Mark raised his head, keeping his fingertips pressed to Uncle Joe's throat. "Does anyone know CPR?"

Everyone around them stood stiff, not even moving enough to shake their heads.

"I hope I'm doing this right," Mark muttered. "God, help me."

Mark tilted Uncle Joe's head back and pinched his nose. He breathed into Uncle Joe's mouth, backed off enough to quickly inhale another rush of air, then blew into Uncle Joe's mouth a second time.

Remaining on his knees, Mark shuffled a few inches down, flattened his palms on Uncle Joe's chest, and, with straight arms, pushed down onto Uncle Joe's chest. He pumped rapidly ten times, counting as he pumped, blew two more puffs into

Uncle Joe's mouth, and pumped again.

Uncle Joe's body twitched slightly, causing Mark to stop. "Joe!" Mark called into his face; but when no response or further movement happened, Mark continued with the artificial respiration, followed by more pumping.

A woman wearing jeans and a tie-dyed T-shirt covered in paint ran up to Mark. She tossed her purse to the side and dropped to her knees on the opposite side of Uncle Joe from Mark. "I'm a doctor. Heart attack? Has someone called an ambulance?"

"Yes, someone's called."

The woman felt for a pulse. "Nothing," she muttered. She tipped Uncle Joe's head back a little more and pinched his nose. "I'll do mouth-to-mouth, you keep pumping."

"I've never done this before. I don't know how many times."

The woman blew two times into Uncle Joe's mouth. "Two breaths, fifteen pumps. Quickly. Now."

They continued two more repetitions. Halfway through the third repetition, Mark stopped abruptly. His face visibly paled. "I heard a snap. I think I broke something."

Chantelle's stomach churned and she felt faint. If she thought she could get her feet to move, she would have sat down. Instead, she remained where she was, her heart pounding, her head swimming, wondering if she were going to be the next to fall down. "God, please, don't let him die," she whimpered, clutching Mark's laptop like a life preserver.

"Don't stop," the doctor said firmly, but gently. "Right now a cracked rib is the least of his problems."

Even from where she was, Chantelle could see Mark's hands shaking as he once more pressed down onto Uncle Joe's chest and continued, counting from eight to fifteen. As soon as he stopped, the woman blew two more breaths. Mark was just about to resume when suddenly Uncle Joe sputtered. His whole body jerked, and he began to cough. The woman quickly reached to his throat. "We have a pulse!" she called out for all to hear, then raised herself up slightly, remaining low to Uncle Joe's face, but far enough to allow him to focus on her in his weakened condition.

"Stay still, Sir. You've had a heart attack. I'm a doctor. You're at the airport, and an ambulance is on the way. Can you understand me?"

He nodded his head without lifting it from the floor, then visibly sagged. His teeth started chattering.

From the other side, Mark rubbed one hand along Uncle Joe's arm, trying to help restore some circulation, then gripped Uncle Joe's hand. "Joe? It's me. Mark. I'm right here. Everything is going to be okay."

A siren sounded in the distance, coming closer, until Chantelle could see the pulsing red of the lights reflecting on the glass doors leading to the parking lot. Within seconds, the ambulance attendants rushed in, carrying their black bags.

The doctor didn't get up but motioned the attendants to the ground with her. She mumbled some kind of medical jargon while the attendants took Uncle Joe's vital signs. They hurried away, leaving the doctor on the floor, and quickly returned with the portable gurney.

Chantelle watched as they gently moved Uncle Joe onto the thin mattress, strapped him in, and raised the gurney. Aunt Ellen ran to his side, holding his hand while they wheeled him away.

Chantelle stood in silence as the men pushed the gurney through the doorway and into the back of the waiting ambulance. Aunt Ellen scrambled into the back with one of the men, and the ambulance squealed away, lights flashing, siren screaming.

Hank, Leslie, Mark, and Chantelle shuffled to stand closer together, forming a tight-knit circle. Chantelle hadn't noticed the crowd until the moment they began to disperse. Around them, the bustle of the airport resumed as the curious onlookers hurried away, the excitement over. Already, only a minute after the ambulance was gone, it was as if nothing had happened, and everything was back to normal.

Chantelle didn't think her life would ever be normal again.

She and Mark turned at the same time to thank the doctor, but the woman had already disappeared into the crowd.

Above them, a voice blared from the speaker, announcing final boarding for Mark's flight.

Chantelle passed Mark his laptop. "You'd better hurry."

"I can't leave now. I have to know how Joe is. There's always another flight, but there's only one Joe. I'll catch another flight home when I know he's okay."

Leslie glanced toward the door, the last place they'd seen Joe before he disappeared into the ambulance. "I guess they're going to General here in town."

"Excuse me," Chantelle mumbled. "I'll be right back." Without explaining herself, Chantelle ran through the room, quickening her pace when she saw the sign pointing out the location of the washrooms. After relieving herself, she splashed a large handful of cold water on her face and swiped some water into her hair. For lack of anything better to do with her hands, she pressed her palms to the cold aluminum countertop.

She stared at herself in the mirror, but she didn't see her face. All she could see was Mark and the anonymous doctor hunched over Uncle Joe, performing the life-saving CPR.

Uncle Joe.

Chantelle squeezed her eyes shut and once more said a prayer, begging God to spare her uncle's life. While the cold water clung to her face, hot tears seeped from her tightly closed eyes and dripped down her cheeks.

She'd done nothing. In the moment of crisis, she had frozen. All she did was watch, while Mark probably saved her uncle's life.

She'd been totally and utterly useless.

Chantelle opened her eyes and stared at her pathetic reflection.

She wasn't going to make a deal with God. But she could and would make a deal with herself.

Today, she'd failed Uncle Joe. But from here on, she would do anything and everything within her power to help him. She couldn't do anything to help him heal except pray for him, but while he recovered, even if she had to work seven days a week, she would be the best waitress Joe's Diner ever had. Through her work at the restaurant, she would make up to Uncle Joe for her failure today. And that she could promise to Uncle Joe, to herself, and to God.

Chantelle stiffened her posture and ripped a section of paper towel from the dispenser. She blotted her face dry and dabbed her eyes, then marched with confidence and determination to rejoin Mark and his parents. When someone needed help, she would never stand by and do nothing again.

From this moment on, the world would see a new Chantelle Dubois.

five

Mark waited at the ticket counter while the attendant made arrangements to have his suitcase and the box of the diner's business records retrieved from the plane and put into storage at the baggage claim area of the airport until he could come back and retrieve it. On the outside, he stood tall, his demeanor businesslike and professional; inside, he was shaking like a leaf.

Joe.

Joe had almost died. Mark wasn't sure Joe still wouldn't die. Plus, in his efforts to save Joe, Mark had injured him further. The doctor had told him it hadn't mattered, but Mark knew it did. Whatever pain Joe was experiencing in the aftermath of a serious heart attack, Mark had made it worse.

He wished there were something he could do, but the situation was out of his hands.

The attendant hung up the phone. "I'm sorry about your friend, Sir, but I'm sure he's receiving the best medical care now."

Mark turned to look at the glass doors leading to outside, the last place he'd seen Joe as the rear doors of the ambulance shut.

Joe was more than a friend. Because Marella was his age, his family had spent a lot of time with Joe and Ellen as he grew up. He'd spent so much time with them that strangers often thought he and Marella were brother and sister, or at least cousins, when they weren't really related at all, at least not by blood. Since Joe never had a son, on a typical "boys' night out," Mark, his dad, Uncle Jack, and Joe often went to ball games and other such activities together. As a young adult, working at the diner while going to college, he spent more time with Joe than he had with his father, cementing a bond that would never be broken.

He couldn't leave now. Not until he knew Joe would be okay. He turned back to the attendant. "Thank you. I hope so."

"I've made the arrangements for your luggage to be stored for you. At your convenience, just come to the baggage claim area and present two pieces of ID to the agent there, and that's all you need to do. We have another flight with open seats leaving at 10:37 P.M. I can give you a discount because of the nature of why you missed your original flight." Her hands hovered over the keyboard as she waited for his reply.

Mentally counting on his fingers, Mark calculated that with the two-hour time change, the flight would be arriving at just about the right time to get to work in the morning, which he could handle if he had a nap on the plane.

He turned his head and once more looked at the glass doors.

He didn't want to go to work. He wanted to be sure that Joe was going to be okay. Mark wanted to talk to him, to be assured that even though there would be a long recovery period, that everything would be fine—even if it meant staying at the hospital all night. For one day, his boss could go in early to open the office for the rest of the staff, and Darren could handle the students from the local business college. "Thank you, no. I'll rebook later. Thanks for the help with my luggage. Good night."

Mark spun around and joined his parents, who were waiting at the outer perimeter of the check-in area.

"When is your return flight?" his father asked. "Do you have to stay here, or do you want to go back to the house to wait?"

"I didn't book. I want to go to the hospital to see Joe." He turned from his father to his mother. "Do you think he'll be okay?"

His mother tipped her head up. Instead of speaking, her eyes welled up with unshed tears. Beside her, his father stood stark still. Mark could only imagine how worried they were, as their bond of friendship with Joe, like his, went deep.

When his mother finally spoke, her chin quivered and her voice trembled. "I don't know."

Instead of speaking, his father reached over to enclose his mother's hand, giving it a gentle squeeze, and their fingers intertwined.

Mark stared down at their joined hands. The obvious show of affection shouldn't have surprised him. In times of trouble, grief, and especially in times of uncertainty, his parents had each other to lean on.

In that way, all three couples he'd grown up with were the same.

Like his parents, Uncle Jack and Aunt Susan shared the same bond. He knew that his aunt was worried about his uncle, but at least everyone knew his uncle would get better, even if he never gained full mobility in his right leg. Whatever happened, regardless of the outcome, they would always be together.

Even more than his parents or his aunt and uncle, Joe and Ellen often shared the same thoughts. They could finish each other's sentences and often did. They even shared the same quirky sense of humor. Joe and Ellen were two halves of a whole. But unlike his aunt and uncle, no one yet knew if Joe would live or die. In his mind's eye, Mark could see Ellen sitting all alone in the waiting area of the hospital, waiting for news, good or bad. He couldn't imagine what she was going through.

Mark stared absently into the airport crowd. He didn't know why, but his attention centered on those who were coupled together, holding hands as they walked. When one slowed, the other slowed their pace to match. Even when they weren't touching, those coupled together stayed as close together as possible, even in the crowd.

Suddenly, Mark felt incredibly alone.

For the first time in his life, he wondered if somewhere out there was a woman who wasn't necessarily perfect, but was perfect for him—someone who could be as perfect a match for him as the good examples he'd had in his life.

He liked to be organized; at work, he prided himself on his efficiency, and he worked hard. One day he hoped all the extra hours and dedication he put into the company would strengthen his chances for advancement, even a future partnership. Like him, his perfect mate would be focused and calm, an ambitious professional with a good college education and a promising future. Someone with diverse interests, but yet not easily distracted, using sound judgment in all situations, both in business and leisure activities. Visions of Chantelle flashed through his mind. She was everything his ideal was not. Yet, something about her piqued his interest and left him wishing he didn't live so far away.

"Mark! Leslie! Hank! There you are!"

Mark flinched, able to hear Chantelle's voice before he could see her, probably because she was so short.

Just as he was able to pick out her blond hair in the moving crowd, she emerged. "Sorry it took me so long. I accidentally turned the wrong way and then got lost in the crowd. I went back to where I thought the washrooms were to get my bearings, but I must have followed the wrong signs to the wrong washroom and ended up in the other wing of the airport, and I had to ask directions how to get back to the check-in counters and. . ." Her voice trailed off. "I think I'm rambling. Sorry. I'm back. What should we do now?"

"I think we were going to go to the hospital, right, Dad?"

"Yes. Even if we can't see Joe, we shouldn't leave Ellen all alone. At the very least, we should do something about their car. We can't just leave it here. Chantelle, I know you came with Joe and Ellen. You can certainly stay with us until we figure out what to do."

"I'm sure Aunt Ellen will want to stay at the hospital. If someone will drive me back here later, I can get the keys from her and drive the car back to the hospital so she can use it."

"Good idea. Let's get going."

Mark's father drove and his mother sat in the front, leaving Mark to share the backseat with Chantelle.

For the first time since he met her, she was quiet. At first, he found the lack of conversation a welcome change; but as time went on and the silence dragged, the mood in the car became more and more somber. He found himself rolling over worst-case scenarios in his mind, instead of more hopeful thoughts of Joe having a quick and easy recovery.

The more he thought about what had happened and what could happen, the more depressed he became, until he found he wanted to hear Chantelle's cheerful babbling to give him some hope that all could really be well once again. Unfortunately, he didn't know what to say to get her started, so he said nothing.

No one said a word as they parked the car and made their way into the emergency ward. As soon as they identified themselves and asked a few questions, a nurse escorted them to ICU, where they found Ellen in a chair in a small waiting area.

Mark stood back with Chantelle to let his parents talk to Ellen. They had allowed her to see her husband, but only for five minutes. She was now forced to wait for more news as they continued to monitor his condition.

Mark didn't know what he should do, so he walked to the nurse's station and identified himself to see if they would give him an update. Chantelle had followed him, although she remained silent. In addition to being so worried about Joe, Mark wondered if he should also begin to worry about Chantelle being silent so long.

The nurse laid her pencil on the desk and picked up a clipboard. "Mark Daniels and Chantelle Dubois? Normally we wouldn't allow anyone in except for immediate family, but Mr. Dubois has been asking for both of you. He's been quite adamant about it. The doctor has decided it would be better for him to be allowed to see you and say what he wants to say so he can calm down. Please keep your visit to five minutes, then I'm going to ask you both to leave."

Mark's chest tightened as he followed the nurse into Joe's room.

He knew what to expect; but when he actually saw Joe hooked up to all the tubes and wires and monitors, Mark's stomach did a nosedive into his shoes. Behind all the medical accessories and equipment, Joe's complexion was pasty, his eyes were sunken, and his hair lay askew on the pillow, emphasizing his bald spot, which he always tried to keep hidden.

Mark tried clearing his throat, but his voice still wouldn't work.

"Hi, Uncle Joe! You look great!" Chantelle chirped quietly beside him. She shuffled closer and lowered her voice. "Well, maybe not great, but you look better than the last time I saw you."

To give her some credit, Joe opened his eyes and smiled behind the tubes and tape on his face.

Chantelle shuffled closer, grasped the railing, and leaned forward toward him. "How are you feeling? Tell me the truth now."

Joe's voice came out low, scratchy, and barely understandable. "Better than I look, I hear."

"That nice nurse said you wanted to talk to us. You have to make it quick because in four minutes and twelve seconds, they're going to kick us out."

"What am I going to do about the diner?" he choked out, then swallowed hard. "Ellen can't run it. She's never done anything in the diner. Her arthritis. Susan's never worked for the diner, either."

Chantelle reached over to touch his hand. "That's not true. Aunt Ellen makes gallons of that wonderful sauce your burgers are famous for every week."

Joe cleared his throat. "Chantelle, I need you. I know you've been working hard, but I need you to do more. I want you to take over everything that I do. The hosting and the scheduling. I don't want anyone working more than eight hours and killing themselves by working too hard while I'm gone. That means you, too. You understand me?"

Chantelle nodded so fast her hair flopped in her face. "Yes, Uncle Joe. Don't worry."

Joe winced and cleared his throat again. "Mark, I need you to look after things in the kitchen tomorrow until I can figure out what to do there. Jack's still under so much medication, he won't be able to help with any planning."

Mark gulped, knowing the gravity of Joe's request. By asking for him sight unseen earlier, Joe had known Mark wouldn't have left town. "No problem. I can stay a day or two."

Joe smiled slightly, then winced. "Are you sure?"

Mark could well imagine his boss's reaction. As of yet, Sean thought he was once again working through the weekend, when he'd done the exact opposite—he'd left early Friday. At the time, Mark knew that by doing so, he would be making the company miss a number of deadlines on Monday; he'd been willing to accept that responsibility. In fact, Mark had selected clients who wouldn't mind that they were a couple of days late, as justification to take on the students who were coming Monday, whether he was there or not.

In addition to purposely missing deadlines, now he was going to be missing a couple more days without having made prior arrangements and without advance notice.

Mark looked down at Joe. Joe and Uncle Jack always had a plan for the diner that took into consideration the possibility of one of them being gone, but there was no provision for both of them being away at the same time. Possibly, the current staff could have struggled to make an alternate plan, but not without the computer and their entire records system. They'd struggled through the last three days even with Joe there. No one really knew what stock they had on hand, short of going into the storage locker and freezer and physically counting every item by hand.

He didn't know what to suggest.

Mark checked his watch. He could still catch the next flight out. But, if he stayed, within a couple of days, he could have a new computer purchased, all data re-entered, and proper backups made.

If he worked hard, he could be back home and to his job on the third day. Two days off was not going to kill the company, and they couldn't fire him over a few unscheduled days off. However, it probably was going to jeopardize the standing he'd worked so hard to build.

Mark stiffened and forced himself to smile. "No problem. I could use a few days off." Although he could hardly count working two eighteen-hour days for the diner as a vacation.

Joe smiled weakly, showing Mark he'd done the right thing.

The nurse arrived precisely five minutes after they entered the room. "I'm sorry, it's time for you to leave."

Joe closed his eyes. His head sagged back, and he relaxed from head to toe. "Thank you," he muttered. "Nurse, I only need one more thing."

"And what's that, Mr. Dubois?"

"Wheel me down a couple floors to Jack's room. Tonight is our Scrabble night."

"I don't think so, Mr. Dubois." She turned to Mark and Chantelle. "Your time is up. Mr. Dubois needs to rest."

As soon as they left the room and the door closed behind them, Chantelle latched onto Mark's arm.

"He's going to be okay. Did you hear him? He's already joking around about going to see Jack. I wonder if they can move the two of them into the same room. Can you imagine what they'd be like together?"

Mark stared down at her hand, causing her to release her grip. "This is the cardiac ward. Uncle Jack is in postop, and he's still heavily sedated. They wouldn't put them together. And if you don't mind, I'd prefer to hear someone from the

medical profession pronounce Joe's long-term prognosis."
Mark hurried his step. "Excuse me. Nurse? How is he? Is he going to be okay?"

"I can't tell you that, but the doctor can. He's speaking to Mrs. Dubois right now. Please have a seat."

Mark didn't really want to sit down, but he had no choice. As he sat, he noticed that his parents were missing from the small waiting area, so he had to assume that they were with Ellen and the doctor.

As soon as the nurse left, Chantelle immediately started talking.

"That's great that you're going to stay a couple of days. You've made Uncle Joe feel so much better. Once you've got everything in order, I'm sure we can keep things going. I don't imagine it's hard to smile at people and show them to their tables. It might even be fun. The thing that's going to be scary is the ordering. We should be able to tell how much food to order from looking at the old purchase orders. Do you think you can help me find some old purchase orders to use as examples?"

Mark sighed. This was exactly the type of situation he'd had in mind when he'd thought of preparing a database out of the diner's past records. However, it would never have occurred to him that they'd need it immediately. "Everything I need is in the box at the airport. I'll go by and pick it up sometime tomorrow. Until then, I don't know if the current staff would know how to do the ordering. Between Joe and Uncle Jack, they do it all, and they were both very possessive about it. I doubt anything has changed."

"What are we going to do? I don't think they're going to let either one of them out of the hospital by Wednesday to do the week's purchases."

"I can probably get away with staying until late Tuesday night. I should have everything entered in the computer by then. If not, I think I could make an accurate estimate by looking at the present stock. Years ago, Uncle Jack showed me how to estimate quantities and order supplies and do stock when he and Aunt Susan went on vacation. That was also before he put everything on the computer, so we should be okay if I can remember everything. I only did it once. I'll buy a new computer, and I should have it configured and most of the data re-entered before I have to go home."

"That would be great. I've worked in offices all my life and I've done a lot of work on computers. I know I can figure out how to do the payroll. I only wish I knew how long it's going to take, because that will take time from my hosting and serving. The staff's hours are already tight, and now we're going to be a full-time person short. More than a full-time person. Both Jack and Uncle Joe worked more than eight hours a day, sometimes six days a week. I hope the part-time people will be willing to increase their hours. Otherwise, I don't know what I'll do. I'm not exactly sure what Uncle Joe is asking me."

"I'm sure you'll do fine. It sounds like Joe trusts you." Since Chantelle had worked at the restaurant only three days without previous food service experience, Mark wasn't sure that was a wise decision. However, just as he was family to Uncle Jack, she was Joe's family and had only the best interests of the restaurant in mind. That alone would carry her a long way.

Once again, Chantelle's hand found its way to his forearm. "Look! There's the doctor and everyone else." She scrambled to her feet before Mark had a chance to take a breath.

"What did he say? What did he say?" she rattled off as she sprinted toward them.

Mark rose and hurried to join the rest of his family, although he didn't run.

Ellen smiled, immediately easing some of his worry. "It's still too early to tell, but the doctor says that things look very promising. Mark's quick action prevented the damage from being much worse. The doctor said not to worry about Joe's broken rib. He's going to be lying in one spot for a long time, and it's not going to bother him that much. He'll be on lots of painkillers for awhile. But with sufficient rest, losing some weight, and starting an exercise program, the doctor says he can make a full recovery."

Mark sagged in relief. "That's great," he said with a sigh.

Chantelle clasped her hands in front of her and did a little hop. "Praise God!" she chimed.

"What do we do now?" Mark asked.

His father stepped forward. "I don't think there's anything we can do. The doctor said Joe has to rest, but Ellen wants to stay for a bit and see him again later. We've called Marella. She's on her way, and we can leave as soon as she gets here."

"But what about the car?" Chantelle asked. "It's still at the airport."

"I never thought of that. I guess we can take you to the airport and you can drive it home."

Chantelle shook her head. "I don't want to leave Aunt Ellen without the car. But if I leave it at their house, then I won't have a way to get home." She paused. One eye closed, she raised her fist to her chin and tapped her finger to her cheek. "I know! How about if we all go to your house and drop you and Leslie at home, then Mark can drive me to the airport. He can even pick up his luggage while we're there. If we both drive back to Aunt Ellen's house, I can drop off the car, and Mark can drive me home, then he can go back to your place for the night."

His parents simply stared at her. Ellen stared blankly at the wall.

Mark blinked a few times and recounted the stages Chantelle outlined. "It's a lot of driving," he said, "but it will work."

His father shook his head. "As long as you say so. There's Marella."

six

"Mom! What happened? How's Dad? Can I see him?"

Chantelle stood back as Marella gave her mom a big, tearful hug. At her daughter's touch, Aunt Ellen's tears once more began to flow. "They're still watching him, although they say the danger appears to be over. They're going to observe him for twenty-four hours, then they've got a bunch of tests to run while he rests and heals. They didn't tell me how long he's going to be here; but after that, when he gets home, he's got to rest some more and get back on his feet slowly and under supervision."

"So he's going to be okay?"

"Yes. Praise God, he's going to be okay."

They all exchanged hugs of relief and said their good-byes. Leaving Marella with Aunt Ellen, they began the first leg of their journey, which was the trip to Mark's parents' house.

Now that she knew Uncle Joe would get better, Chantelle allowed herself to relax. Instead of dwelling on the daunting task of trying to organize things at the restaurant, she kept conversation on insignificant things, mostly on the weather and the upcoming baseball game.

"We're home," Leslie said as they pulled into the driveway. "Would you like to come in for a few minutes? I can put on a pot of coffee. It's been quite a day, and you might want to relax for a bit before doing all that driving. It will only take a few minutes."

Mark nodded. "Great idea. I'd love one."

Chantelle shook her head. "I'd better not. We're going to be driving and driving, with nowhere to stop for a long time, if you know what I mean."

63

Mark smirked. "Oh. I never thought of that. Chantelle is right. We do have a lot of miles to make, and it's already getting late. You'd better give me the key. It will be late by the time I get back, and I don't want to disturb you."

"That's true. Just leave the key on the kitchen table when you get home. What should we do about cars tomorrow? Your mother and I need both cars to get to work. It's getting too late to phone someone else to hitch a ride."

Chantelle leaned forward and stuck her head in the space between the two front seats. "Don't worry. I can come by and pick Mark up in the morning on my way to the diner." She leaned back in the seat, turning to face Mark. "That is, if you don't mind being early. We open at six-thirty, so I have to be there at six-fifteen to get the coffee started."

"I hope you have a key for the restaurant."

She patted her purse. "Actually, I do. Uncle Joe said sometimes I might get there before him and he didn't want me waiting outside all alone."

"That sounds like Joe."

As soon as Mark got the house key from his parents, they were on their way.

As Mark drove, Chantelle filled him in on everything she'd been able to absorb in her three days of working at the diner, which she didn't think was very much. She listened intently when he told her what he remembered from his years of working in the kitchen. They shared a laugh and a few smiles, seeing that not much had changed in the years since Mark had been away, including Brittany, Mark's distant cousin.

They pulled into the airport parking lot, and Mark stopped in front of the baggage claim area so he could run in and get his suitcase and the box of receipts.

"This should only take a minute. I'll do my best to hurry," Mark said before he slammed the door shut.

While he ran inside, Chantelle slid into the driver's seat and kept the car idling in the loading zone. She started to get nervous when several minutes had passed and Mark had still not reappeared. At last, he came, empty-handed, through the automatic doors.

"They don't know where my luggage is." His voice sounded more like a growl as he slid into the passenger seat and shut the door. "Doesn't that take the cake? The agent assured me, though, that it has to be somewhere in the airport. They said I could wait while they located it, or they'd call me as soon as it was found. I'm too bushed to stick around any longer. I'll come back when they phone to say it's in hand."

"Are you sure?" Chantelle couldn't tell by looking at him if he was just being polite and leaving on her account. "I don't mind waiting."

"I'm sure. I've had my fill of airports for today. Let's go get Joe's car. Where is it?"

Chantelle pointed to a lamppost on the far side of the lot. "It was much busier than this at suppertime. Do you know this is the third time in three days that I've been here?"

"Me, too, Chantelle."

"Oh. That's right." Chantelle shook her head. "But that's different. It doesn't count when you're getting off or on a plane."

"I didn't get back on. Remember?"

"Never mind. I'll see you back at Uncle Joe's house. Do you remember how to get there from here?"

"I should, but it's been a number of years since I've lived here, and it's now dark out. I'd better follow you. Drive carefully, and no speeding."

Fortunately, the ever-darkening evening light kept Mark from seeing her blush. She didn't usually speed, but she'd just gotten a ticket a couple of weeks ago because she had been late leaving for a job interview and foolishly tried to make up the time by driving too fast. In the end, she didn't get the job, which added insult to injury. However, now she was glad she didn't, because now she was available to help Uncle Joe when he needed it.

She raised her hand and held up her first three fingers, giving him the "scout's honor" sign. "No speeding. I promise," she said as she walked toward the car.

She waved to Mark, then drove toward the exit, hoping and praying she had enough money in her wallet to cover the cost of the extended time the car spent in the lot. Fortunately, she had a quarter to spare after the fee was paid, saving her the embarrassment of having to ask Mark, who was behind her in the short lineup, for money. She was almost afraid to look at the gas gauge; but to her relief, it read half full.

Chantelle took advantage of the half-hour journey to think of the days ahead.

She didn't know what Uncle Joe expected of her. She'd been a disaster in the kitchen, of that there had been no doubt. Her waitressing skills were questionable, but adequate, although she would do better if the restaurant used plastic tableware.

Hosting was probably the task for which she was most suited. Dealing cheerfully with people was what she did best. However, since the diner was a small family restaurant, the job involved more than simply chatting with people, showing them to their table, and handing out menus.

The promise she made in the airport washroom echoed through her head. She could never have foreseen that Uncle Joe would need her to step into his shoes and run the diner. Her hands shook on the steering wheel as she contemplated the magnitude of her promise. She hadn't had time to think about it or pray before accepting her new responsibilities. They had been cast upon her without warning or preparation.

She had learned in Sunday school that God didn't give a person more than they could handle. She wouldn't have thought she could do it, but God must have thought her capable of rising to the challenge. Since she'd actually spent some time serving, she thought she could manage the front operations. She didn't foresee any problems in doing the payroll or banking, as those were extensions of office procedures she'd done

in other jobs. Nor did she see that she would have any difficulty in working the cash register and processing the credit
card transactions.

As to the kitchen, after her one day of disasters, all she
could do was trust that Kevin could help, because she was
well beyond her capabilities there. For the next two days, she
would take advantage of Mark's presence. Then she would
pray really hard until Uncle Joe and Jack could return or at
least provide a little assistance and advice.

Her fears and misgivings about the situation didn't matter.
Before she frightened herself into failure, she told herself that
she would take her new responsibilities one day at a time.
One hour at a time, if need be.

She didn't have to worry about the food order until Wednesday. For the next two days, Mark would be spreading his time
between fixing up the information in the computer and helping Kevin to learn to manage the kitchen. He wasn't leaving
until Tuesday night. Tomorrow was Monday, and Monday
had enough worries of its own.

Taking things one step at a time, the second step of tonight's
task was now over. She pulled into Uncle Joe's driveway,
waited for the garage door to go up, and then drove inside to
park the car for the night.

Once she had the car parked in the correct position, she hit
the button to close the garage, slammed the car door shut, and
ran as fast as she could, ducking under the garage door as it
closed. Not being as fast as she had hoped, she scraped her
back a little bit on her way out; but she did make it without
the door flattening her to the ground, which she thought quite
an accomplishment.

Mark quickly appeared beside her. "Are you all right? What
in the world do you think you're doing?"

Chantelle grinned from ear to ear. "I haven't done that since
I was a kid. Believe it or not, I was shorter then. I didn't want
to set the alarm off, so I couldn't go through the house because

I don't know the code. This was the only way to get out, the way I came."

"You could have taken the remote control into the driveway and closed it from outside without having to play Russian roulette with the door crashing down on you."

"It didn't crash down on me. It just nudged me a little bit. I couldn't take the remote out of the car. If I did, what would I do with it? Take it home? What if Aunt Ellen wanted to go somewhere? She wouldn't be able to close the garage. Aunt Ellen can't hit the switch and run through the garage and beat the door like I can."

Mark craned his neck to check behind her. He brushed something on the back of her blouse with his fingertips, then wiped his fingers on his pants. "The jury is still out as to whether or not you beat the door, but I don't want to argue with you. Let's go. Next stop, your place. You'll definitely have to give me directions." Mark stifled a yawn. "How long is it going to take to get there?"

"About half an hour. And then it's going to take you about three-quarters of an hour to get back to your parents' house."

Mark groaned. "Let's not stand here, then."

On their way once again, Chantelle gave Mark general directions as he made his way to the main road.

While he drove, she told him that she'd been thinking about what the next few days would bring; and now that she had some time to think properly, she wasn't so nervous. He seemed happy to hear that she thought, with Kevin's help, the two of them would be able to keep the supplies at optimum levels for the coming weeks.

The farther they went, the less Mark spoke. They still had about fifteen minutes' worth of driving to do, when Mark stifled another yawn.

"I'm so sorry, Mark. I should have waited and let your mom make us coffee. I forgot that your body clock still says that it's two hours later. It's been such a horrible day. You've also done so much work this weekend. You must be exhausted."

This time, he couldn't stifle his yawn. "Thanks for reminding me."

"Sorry. We're almost there."

Rather than yap his ear off, Chantelle turned up the volume on the CD player, which fortunately was playing a rousing praise chorus. When Mark didn't respond to the encouraging words, she told herself that he was simply too tired to enjoy the song properly.

"Here we are. It's that duplex over there with the red mailbox. I'm on the left."

He simply nodded and pulled into the driveway. "Good night, Chantelle."

"I know you don't want to be reminded, but you look so tired. It's no trouble at all for me to make a small pot of coffee and give you one for the road."

He raised his arms over his head and stretched. "You know, I think I'll take you up on that. Besides, I think it will do me some good to stretch my legs. I feel like I've been driving for hours."

"You *have* been driving for hours."

"You're just so full of encouraging reminders tonight, aren't you?"

She couldn't tell if he was kidding, so she let his comment go without responding.

He followed her into the kitchen, but instead of sitting at the table, he remained standing while she put the coffee on. It was just as well. He was less likely to fall asleep on his feet than if he were sitting down. If it were possible, he looked even more tired than when he first arrived on Friday. Her heart went out to him, knowing that for at least a few days, things wouldn't get much better. At least when he went home on Tuesday night, he would be able to catch up on his sleep once he got back to his normal routine.

"Remember, I'll be picking you up about six. I'm sorry if that makes you get up earlier than if you were driving yourself."

"Only fifteen minutes. Which reminds me. With the time change, five-thirty A.M. is too late for me to phone my boss and tell him I won't be in. I'm usually there at seven, which is five here. I won't even be awake by then. I know it's almost midnight at home, but I had better phone now instead of waiting until morning. Sean's got to go in to work early to open the office door for the rest of the staff."

He reached into his pocket for his cell phone, pushed the button, and waited for it to be ready to dial.

"You're going to call your boss from your cell phone? What about the roaming charges?"

His brows knotted as he watched the phone. "The bill won't be a big deal, but it looks like I forgot to charge my battery before I left home. I won't have enough power to complete the call. Do you mind if I use your phone?"

Chantelle didn't want to think of the additional long-distance charges on her phone bill. However, she reminded herself that she now had a real job and could actually pay the phone bill on time. If Mark cut his call short, the long-distance charges wouldn't be much more than the late fee she would have paid anyway. "I don't mind. Make your call."

seven

Mark recalled Sean's home number from the memory on his cell phone, barely managing to jot it down before the display window went blank.

"Good timing," he muttered.

He dialed the number, hoping Sean hadn't gone to bed yet. Being nearly ten at night was bad enough for Mark after a long day; but for Sean, it was nearly midnight.

At the second ring, Mark's stomach started to churn.

Sean answered on the third ring.

"Hi, Sean. It's Mark. I won't be in to work tomorrow. Actually, I won't be in Tuesday, either. I'll probably be back Wednesday; but at this point, I'm not sure."

"What's the matter? Are you sick? You sound okay."

"I'm calling from the coast, actually. I left Friday night and I've been here ever since. I'm in the middle of a family emergency, and I need to stay for a few days."

"You left Friday? What about the Kowalski contract? And Shaben's?"

Instead of feeling guilty, Mark found himself starting to bristle. If his boss had been at the office Friday, working instead of out playing golf, then Sean would have noticed that Mark left early. If he was so inclined, Sean could also have pitched in to help meet the deadlines he'd promised unreasonably instead of expecting Mark to come in and work all weekend. "Darren is more than capable of handling those jobs Monday morning," he said, extending his levels of patience in order to sound polite.

"Those jobs aren't Darren's. They're yours."

The difference between himself and Darren doing the same

work was that when done after hours or on the weekend, they would have to pay Darren overtime wages, and Mark was expected to do it as part of his salary. "I'm being honest with you, Sean. If I had called in sick, you would have thought nothing of giving those files to Darren. I've also got a couple of students coming in from the career college tomorrow morning. They'll help ease the workload in exchange for minimal job experience and training."

"You shouldn't be taking this time off. We need you here. Can't you get an earlier flight?"

Mark noticed the little part about "family emergency" went right over Sean's head. On purpose, no doubt. As far as the family was concerned, not only did his uncle Jack need him more than ever, now so did Joe. "I probably could, but I'm not going to. I'm quite entitled to take some time off."

"We have someone off on holidays every week for the next three months. We need you here."

Aside from the volume of files on his desk, which over the last six months hadn't been any different from any other day, nothing was particularly critical. Everything on his desk had only the usual client deadlines.

"That doesn't matter, as long as I'm not off at the same time as Darren. In fact, as senior supervisor, I should have taken my vacation first. Let me remind you that I'm entitled to take the whole week off if I want to. I'm entitled to three weeks this year, and I don't see a good reason why I can't take all of them right now."

"You can't have three weeks off. Right now, I can't give you one week. I want you back at work Tuesday morning unless someone has passed away."

Something snapped in Mark's brain. Joe had nearly died at the airport. Even though the doctor called his progress "promising," Joe had far from a clean bill of health. While Uncle Jack would definitely recover, he was far from able to resume work. He was still on such heavy painkillers that he couldn't form two coherent sentences in a row. Mark had hoped to stay at least until both his uncle and Joe were released from the hospital.

"No one has 'passed away'," Mark spat out. "But I'm still staying. In fact, I changed my mind about when I'll be back. I'm taking a whole week."

Sean's voice dropped to a low growl. "You can't do that. I'm warning you. I'll give you the two days, but that's it."

Since Mark hadn't preauthorized any vacation time, he knew Sean didn't have to give it to him. However, nothing on his desk specifically needed his personal attention to the exclusion of any other staff member. With a little help from Darren, the two students surely would be able to accomplish what Mark could alone, in an eight-hour day.

The only thing Mark felt was the stab of intimidation rather than the necessity of keeping his clients' files current. The issue was no longer the work that needed to be done.

The issue had become control. Suddenly, Mark saw himself being used as a pawn in a game where he wasn't allowed to know the rules. Over the years, he had found himself so buried in one problem after another, he hadn't seen what was happening around him. Now, from a distance, his perspective had changed. He could see the situation as it really was.

"You know, Sean, come to think of it, I haven't taken a vacation for the last two years, so there's another four weeks you owe me, besides this year's three weeks."

"We're really too busy for you to have time off. You won't be able to make it back for morning, so I want you back Tuesday. Take your vacation another time."

"This isn't about a vacation in the tropics. I said it was a family emergency."

"Tuesday, Mark."

Mark stiffened from head to toe, suddenly feeling conviction unlike anything else he'd ever experienced in his life. Sean had done whatever he could, including empty promises and deceit, even lies, to have Mark do what he wanted, regardless of what Mark was entitled to and regardless of the strain on Mark's personal life or his health, working unreasonably long hours, seven days a week, to say nothing of the on-the-job stress. All for his own gain. Business was business, but Sean had long ago crossed the line.

"I want what you've promised, and now is the time I'm calling you on it. Starting tomorrow, I'm taking my seven weeks of paid vacation. I also seem to recall you promising me equivalent time off for all the weekends I've worked. I could tally up all those weekends if you want me to. In writing. Plus, in four years, I've only taken two sick days, which means you either have to give me twenty-two days off or the equivalent pay. I think that's got to add up to, oh. . ." He let his voice trail off as he calculated an approximate total. "Four and a half months, just guessing on the weekends, of course."

"Four months!" At Sean's shouting, Mark held the phone away from his ear and winced.

Mark cleared his throat. "Four and a *half* months," he said, emphasizing the "half." "But it's probably more. That's just an estimate. I think I'll take five." He left the next question unsaid, but definitely hanging. *So what are you going to do about it?*

"I have to take that to the board."

"No, you don't. You're senior partner. I report directly to you and to you alone."

A long pause hung over the line. Mark's stomach tied in knots. He waited for Sean's next words, which would either be a demand of a specific date to return—attached to an "or else"—or simply a blunt "you're fired."

"I hope whatever it is you're doing is worth it."

The bang of Sean slamming the phone down in his ear ended the phone call, making Mark flinch. Numbly, he listened to the even buzz of the dial tone, still not entirely believing what had just transpired.

In slow motion, he replaced the handset to the receiver and turned around. Chantelle stood in the doorway between the kitchen and the hallway, her eyes as wide as they could go, her splayed fingers covering her wide-open mouth.

"I think he just hung up on me," he mumbled, his boss's last words replaying in his mind like an endless loop tape.

"Oh, Mark. . . ," Chantelle mumbled between her fingers. "What have you done?"

Mark grinned weakly. "I'm not really sure."

In the blink of an eye, Chantelle stood in front of him. Before he could figure out what she was doing, she reached forward, wrapped her fingers around his, and looked up at him. Her big blue eyes filled with such sadness, he wondered if she were going to cry. "I'm so sorry, Mark. I feel like this is my fault. If Uncle Joe thought I could take care of things, he wouldn't have asked you to stay for a few days, and you wouldn't have lost your job."

He shrugged his shoulders, but she only held on tighter at his movement. "Technically, Sean didn't actually say I was fired. Regardless, I'm not going to let him intimidate me anymore. Please, don't think any of this was your fault. The decision to stay longer was my own. I'm not going anywhere until both Joe and Uncle Jack are ready to go back to work."

She gave his fingers a little squeeze, then let his hands go. Mark expected her to back up, but instead she stepped forward. Suddenly, her hands wormed between his arms and his waist. She flung herself toward him, wrapped her arms around him, and hugged him tight. "That's so sweet," she mumbled, with her face pressed against his chest.

Mark stood stiff, his arms slightly raised behind her back, not knowing what to do. He hadn't given up his job because he was being "sweet." He did it because Joe and Uncle Jack needed him.

He waited for her to back up, but she didn't. She remained pressed against him, giving him no sign that she intended to release him anytime soon.

Cautiously, Mark lowered his arms until his palms brushed against her back. At his touch, instead of shying away or backing up, she snuggled into him even more and squeezed him tighter, encouraging him not only to relax, but to hug her back. So he did.

As he held Chantelle as snugly as she held him, her warmth seeped into him, revitalizing him.

He couldn't remember anyone ever calling him sweet before, if anyone ever had. The only other person in the universe who might have said such a thing would have been his mother, so long ago he didn't want to think about it.

Mark remembered his mother's hugs when he was a child. Chantelle's arms around him felt nothing like his mother's. Yet at the same time, Chantelle's hug wasn't the same as the last time he'd had a girlfriend and they'd embraced each other before they kissed. He was positive Chantelle had no intention of kissing him.

Normally, he wouldn't have considered himself a huggy-type person, but he didn't want to let go. It felt too good. He wanted to believe that Chantelle's spontaneous response meant everything that it implied—that not only did she think he had made the right decision, but that she would support him in what he needed to do to make his current situation work.

Mark couldn't help himself. Even though he knew he was too tired to think properly and that he shouldn't trust his own judgment, he lowered his head and nuzzled his face into her hair. The fragrance of some kind of apple-scented shampoo filled his senses—sweet, yet tangy at the same time, just like Chantelle.

Before he thought about the ramifications of what he was doing, he buried his face farther and gently kissed the top of her head.

Suddenly, she stiffened in his arms. He wasn't ready to let the moment end, but he wouldn't hold her against her will.

Chantelle backed up a few steps, blinked a few times, and looked up at him from a safe distance. "So what are you going to do?"

Mark swiped his hair back and rammed his hands into his pockets. "It looks like I just got myself a new job in the kitchen at Joe's Diner."

∂

Mark lowered himself into the passenger seat of Chantelle's low-slung economy import car and fastened the seatbelt. "You're five minutes late."

"I'm not late. I said I'd be here 'about' six. I think five minutes after six still qualifies as 'about'. Did you sleep well?"

He smiled as Chantelle shifted into first gear and the car started moving. "Strangely, yes, I did." He'd fallen asleep with a smile on his face, feeling at peace with himself for the first time since he had been awarded his management position at S&B Accounting. From that day forward, he'd never been able to keep up with the ever-increasing expectations heaped on his shoulders, no matter how hard he tried. For awhile, at least, he wouldn't have to deal with the unending pressure, although now he would face expectations of another kind. These new expectations, however, he could deal with because he no longer felt completely alone. Even though he hadn't slept that many hours, the sleep he did get refreshed him like never before. "And you? Did you sleep well?"

"No, I didn't. Are you really not going home on Tuesday night? You're really staying?"

"Yes, I'm staying."

She remained facing forward as she pulled into the traffic on the main road. "I don't understand why you're doing this. You're a CPA. You've got a fancy college education and a great management job in a high-rise office tower downtown in a real city. Why are you jeopardizing that to be a temporary helper in a little family-owned and -operated restaurant out here in the middle of nowhere?"

"Actually, I'm beyond a CPA; I've got my MBA. And I'm not jeopardizing anything. Employed or not, I still have my certificate. . .although I think I'll have to get someone to take it off the wall and mail it to me." He pulled his electronic organizer out of his pocket and jotted himself a reminder.

"But it was such a good job. How can you just give it up like that? Can't you phone your boss and tell him you were just kidding or having a bad day or something like that?"

Mark's smile faded. "I don't mind playing the game; but if I'm going to play the game, I want to know the rules. I just found out that I don't like the rules."

A charged silence hung in the air, but Mark waited for her response.

"This is so hard for me to accept. You're just throwing that good, well-paying, high-prestige job away. I've been looking for a job for months. I'm so desperate that I'll take anything. I think Uncle Joe felt sorry for me, and that's the only reason he gave me this job. I'm really not suited to waitressing."

Not wanting to spoil the moment, Mark didn't confirm her statement. "What did you do at your last job? Do you mind my asking why you're no longer still there?"

"It was just a simple data-entry office job. I got phased out with increasing technology and better programs. What I'd really like to do is work as a bank teller. But there's another job that's being phased out. The more bank machines we see, the fewer tellers they need."

"That's the cost of progress, I guess. Why don't you go back to school and upgrade your education?"

"Unfortunately, that takes money I don't have. For now, I'm just grateful to have this job and make it from day to day."

Mark never had to worry about money. While attending college, he'd only worked part-time to cover a few personal expenses. His parents had paid for his tuition and his room and board, as long as he paid for his books. They'd even given him a rather beat-up car, but it had four wheels and got him where he needed to go. The only time he'd been without a job was when he finished his last year at the university to get his master's degree, which he'd been able to do because he had enough money saved after living at home.

Again, Mark pulled out his organizer. He made himself a note to do something special for his parents to thank them for making it so easy for him to get ahead in life—if he could count spending the last four years of his life slaving for Sean as "getting ahead." But that situation had been of his own making and not his parents' fault.

He put the entry into the memory and tucked the unit back into his pocket.

"Hopefully they'll call from the airport and tell me that the box of the diner's records and my suitcase have been found and are ready for pickup at the baggage claim office some-time this afternoon. I'll buy a few more things until I can get someone to go into my apartment and pack enough for me to get by for a few months and ship it out to me. Do you know where I should go to lease a car? Or maybe I should pay someone to drive my car here for me. I wonder if I could find someone who needs an apartment to sublet for a few months. I'm not going to give up my apartment, but it seems wasteful and not very safe to leave it vacant for so long. At least I've got my computer with me." Once again, he pulled out his organizer and made himself a few notes.

They pulled into the parking lot, and both exited the car at the same time.

Chantelle closed her door, but remained standing with her fingertips pressed onto the car window. "You really intend to stay for five months, don't you?"

Mark stood beside the car and also pushed the door closed. The scrape of metal on metal groaned while the door was in motion. When it came to a stop, the alignment between the door and the car body was out by half an inch, and the interior light remained shining.

Chantelle grinned sheepishly over the car roof. "It's an old car. You have to slam it."

If he wasn't mistaken, Chantelle's car was the same kind he'd owned when he was in college, even the same year, which didn't say much for Chantelle's car. Still, for its age, it wasn't in bad condition, unless someone had to use the passenger door. Yesterday he wondered why Joe had been so insistent about picking Chantelle up for church. He now began to wonder if Joe knew something about Chantelle's car that he didn't.

Mark reopened the door, but he didn't close it. Over the past few minutes, the sky had lightened. The sun had not yet broken the horizon, but the sky had come aglow with the pending sunrise. The fresh air and clear sky hinted at a beautiful day to come.

He had wanted to be out of the house and to the diner early so he could talk to Chantelle before they both got buried in the business of the day. Because of the subject matter, he didn't feel it best to detract from her concentration while driving through the early morning rush-hour traffic. Now, the beauty of the morning sunrise somehow made the parking lot the perfect place to say what needed to be said.

Mark lowered his laptop case and leaned it against the rear tire. He then shuffled closer to the car, rested his elbows on the roof, and clasped his hands together. "I've been thinking about what Joe said at the hospital. Now that I'm staying, that changes things."

Chantelle also stepped closer to the car. Leaning forward, she curled her fingers over the roof and raised herself up on her tiptoes. Her chin barely touched the edge of the roof of her car. "What do you mean?"

Leaving both elbows planted on the roof, Mark lifted one arm and rested his chin on top of his fist. "Joe asked you to take over for him, which means looking after the servers and doing the hosting and taking in the receipts. He asked me to run the kitchen and do Uncle Jack's other duties while I'm here, because that's something you can't do. Now that I'm staying, with both of us looking after things, I would think they'll be in no rush to come back before they're ready, which is a good thing. So I think we should talk about working together."

Chantelle backed up so she no longer touched the car, putting more distance between them. She crossed her arms over her chest. "Working together? You and me? Us? For how long?"

Mark quickly slammed the car door closed, picked up his laptop, and jogged around the car to talk to her without anything between them.

"For as long as it takes. We don't want either Joe or Uncle Jack endangering their health by coming back too soon." He held his free hand toward her, inviting her to shake on it and seal the deal in a gentleman's agreement. "What do you think? Partners?"

She stared down at his hand like it was made of toxic waste. "I don't know what to say. This is all so sudden. A couple of days ago, I was just waitressing, and now Uncle Joe has given me the responsibility to run the place."

A lump formed in Mark's stomach. He hadn't expected her to jump for joy at his proposal, but he had expected her reaction to be a little more positive. He wondered if maybe she now regretted what passed between them last night, although he hadn't quite yet figured out exactly what had happened or why. All he did know was when Chantelle hugged him, his whole world shifted.

For the first time in a very long time, even though it had only been a few minutes, he had someone he could lean on when he was down. For the last few years, he'd become less and less satisfied with the way his life was going, yet he couldn't do anything to change it. Lately, he felt even God had deserted him. He felt lost, with nowhere to turn. Now, stepping in to help keep the diner afloat in Joe and Uncle Jack's absence could be the one thing to give him some direction again.

"You can't possibly be more caught off guard than I am with everything that's happened in the last few days. I'm not even sure I have a job to go back to. Either way, I want to be as much help as I can be. I'm sure Joe and Uncle Jack would want it that way."

She looked up at him, straight into his eyes.

Mark's breath caught. Chantelle's eyes were like a gateway to her soul. Uncertainty shimmered in the blue depths. He could see the questions flickering through her mind, wondering if she were doing the right thing, even down to questioning her ability. Yet, at the same time, he could see her resolve, that she had accepted this responsibility. Even though she wasn't sure what she was doing, she would do it to the best of her ability or go down trying.

Running a restaurant would be a daunting task. Fortunately, despite everything he saw in her eyes, he did not see fear of what lay ahead. That, at least, was comforting. He had enough doubts of his own without adding fear to the mixture of uncertainty and inexperience. He would like to think they could form a good partnership, but in reality, he had limited experience in the restaurant industry, and she had even less.

The bottom line was that she needed him. Likewise, in a strange way, he felt he needed her; but he couldn't figure out why. She had no experience as a business entrepreneur. He'd never met anyone so accident-prone. Her constant cheerfulness and boisterous personality sometimes made him want to hit his head against the wall.

Once again, the unbidden thought that desperate times called for desperate measures ran through his head, making him feel like he was sinking deeper and deeper into a realm beyond his control. With both Uncle Jack and Joe unable to work, the situation at the restaurant had become critical. He didn't have the experience to run the diner, nor did Chantelle. The scary thing was that, together, he and Chantelle were Uncle Jack and Joe's only hope of keeping the diner running until their return. At least he had some experience in the kitchen. He could only hope she proved to be a fast learner and adapted quickly.

For now, though, he would take each day one step at a time—one hour at a time if he had to.

Mark cleared his throat. "I'm not asking you to marry me. I'm only asking that we work together as partners until Joe and Uncle Jack are ready to come back. You don't want to see the business fall apart after all the years and hard work they put into it, do you?"

Chantelle stiffened, not breaking eye contact. Her face lost any hint of uncertainty or hesitation as she slid her hand in his and held on, catching him off guard with the firmness of her grip.

Mark closed his hand around hers. While his fingers wrapped almost around her whole hand, her tiny fingers barely curved around the width of his palm. His hand completely enveloped hers, like holding the hand of a child. Yet in that childlike hand, he felt strength and, most important, determination.

"Okay," she said with one firm up-and-down motion of their hands. "Partners."

Mark stared down at their hands. His feeble return of her handshake was nothing short of pitiful. "Partners," he muttered.

She pulled her hand out of his. Immediately he felt the coolness of the morning air on his palm, almost making him shiver with the loss of the warm contact.

Chantelle turned toward the diner. Not knowing what else to do while he tried to organize his addled brain, Mark rammed his hand into his pocket and turned as well.

"There it is," she sighed. "Joe's Diner."

Mark studied the small building. The restaurant hadn't

changed much over the years—probably the last time any major renovations had been done was fifteen years ago, when Mark was in middle school. The end building of a small neighborhood community mall, Joe's Diner was wider than the other businesses in the structure, its construction being a big square added onto the side of a rectangle that comprised the rest of the small strip mall. Large windows covered the three visible, unattached sides of the diner, allowing passers-by to see the fifties-style curtains hung all around, but no further inside, which offered the patrons privacy as they ate.

The main door was flush with the walls, but an archway had been added to the front of the building, creating a short tunnel-like entranceway, giving the otherwise plain building a unique shape. Above the curve of the arch, an oversized neon sign blazed the words *Joe's Diner* in brilliant yellow and navy blue.

Above the roof, the sky continued to brighten from yellow to pale pink to hues of purples and blues until the brilliance of the sun finally appeared.

Chantelle stepped away from him. "Here goes nuthin'. In we go."

Mark walked behind Chantelle as she jogged to the entrance and unlocked the door. While she ran to shut off the alarm, the *beep beep beep* of the warning signal counted down the thirty seconds allowed to disarm the system.

"When you go to the airport, can you make me a key on your way back?" he called out as soon as the beeping stopped.

She returned to him, coming to a stop directly in front of him, and thrust the keys into his hand. "It's your suitcase. You can go to the airport. And while you're out, you can also go to the wholesaler and pick up a few things we need. Uncle Joe says that Jack always makes a trip to the wholesaler on Monday to stock up on the things they have in low supply after the weekend. They place the big order Wednesday, and it's delivered Thursday."

Mark stared at her. If she already knew something of the

operation, maybe, just maybe, things wouldn't be so bad after all. If he could keep her away from anything breakable, they might actually have a chance.

Her biggest problem would be difficulty in being taken seriously as a manager, both by customers and staff. He'd dealt with a lot of people in management positions over the past four years, many of them women. Chantelle didn't fit into anything close to the mold. For one thing, she was too. . .cute.

The woman barely topped five feet. Mark wondered if she weighed much over a hundred pounds. What she lacked in size, though, she more than made up for with hair. The first time he saw her was at the end of a hectic day. Her hair had been flattened in a most unflattering way by being confined in a bandanna for the previous twelve hours. Saturday she'd worn it barely held together with more clips than he'd ever seen a woman use at one time. Sunday, for church, a fluffy ponytail holder held a wad of her hair straight up from the center of her head, then flopping over to one side. Until now, he hadn't seen it in its full, unencumbered glory.

Today, with her hair wild and free, he could almost compare Chantelle and her mass of curls to a dandelion, ready and waiting for someone to make a wish. Regardless of how she wore her hair, her full cheeks gave her a more youthful appearance than her years. He knew she was close to his own age; but if she weren't careful with her clothing and makeup, she could easily have been mistaken for twenty-two.

He hoped that today she had those same hair clips in her purse and intended to install them as soon as she had time. Learning more about her each time they met, he suspected her lack of attention to controlling her hair had more to do with an inability to organize herself properly in the morning than with her hair being that unmanageable.

He could almost draw a parallel between the wild disorganization of her hair and the work habits he'd seen thus far.

He'd seen her dealing with people, both those she knew and

those whom she didn't. It was in her job to be cheerful to the clientele; but when she laughed, he could hear her clear across the room. Often, when she was en route to the kitchen, he heard her before he saw her. In response, people were already smiling by the time she arrived.

Her constant cheerfulness would be the only thing that could save her. If she could keep it up. He suspected she had no idea what she was in for in the days and weeks to come.

Mark tucked Chantelle's keys into his pocket. He repeated a few times in his head that if Joe trusted her, he had to trust her, too.

"I guess I can find a map or get directions to the wholesaler's warehouse. I'm going to assume Uncle Jack and Joe have an account and I won't have to write a check, because I don't even know where they keep the checks yet." He smacked his palm to his forehead and ran his hand down his face. "Even if we did have checks, they're no good to us. Neither of us has signing authority."

"I'll phone the bank and ask what we can do. I don't know if I want to think of what other problems we're going to face in the next few days, do I?"

Mark looked down at her. "Before we do anything, we have to talk about what we're going to say to the rest of the staff." He checked his watch. "I think we have seven minutes before someone walks in the door."

She nodded, making her hair bounce. "Yes. And there's something else we should be doing, too."

"What?"

"We have to pray."

Mark's chest tightened. After all that had happened in the last few days, Mark had nothing further he wanted to say to God.

eight

Chantelle checked her watch and glanced at the door. "Come on, Mark. We don't have much time. I don't want to rush this."

She waited for him to say something, but Mark failed to show the instant decisiveness Chantelle had come to expect from him.

His hesitation made her wonder if she'd hurt him with her initial reaction before accepting his offer of partnership in running the diner. It was true, he'd caught her by surprise; but the more she thought about it, the more she knew it was a good idea—it was the only way the diner was going to survive, never mind thrive.

In fact, she was getting so excited about having someone with actual experience, to say nothing of a professional business executive pitching in, it was all she could do not to run up and hug him.

That, though, would be a mistake.

She learned the hard way that Mark was not a hugger. After what felt like an eternity of hugging him when he wasn't hugging her back, she'd almost figured out a way to back up and run away with the least amount of embarrassment. Then, to her shock, he actually did hug her back, and with not just a polite, token hug. He'd hugged her back in full measure, making her think that they'd really connected—that he knew without asking that she thought he'd done the right thing.

But, apparently, that wasn't what he thought. Just as she was getting comfortable, maybe even a little too comfortable in his arms, he kissed her. It was only the top of her head, but immediately she knew that she had given him the wrong idea.

Chantelle may have been an eager hugger, but she was not

an eager kisser. She only kissed a man when she meant it. She didn't know Mark well enough to mean anything except business. She reminded herself once again that, even if she did decide she liked him, nothing could ever happen between them. When their uncles returned to work, Mark was going home.

He may have been the "love 'em and leave 'em" type, but Chantelle would never be. She had been on the receiving end of that kind of relationship once, and it was once too often. After living through such an awful experience, she would never do that to anyone else.

She didn't know Mark all that well, but the idea that he could be such a casual Romeo disappointed her. Still, they were going to be working together for a long time, and in that time, she could certainly be friends. At the very least, she could be his Christian sister.

"Mark? Come on. Everyone will be here soon."

"Then we can pray another time," he finally muttered. "It's more important to agree on what we're going to tell the staff."

"I think it's more important to pray. Everyone will understand when it takes awhile for things to fall into place. We need guidance more than anything, I think."

"Guidance," he muttered. "Right."

Chantelle cocked her head and studied Mark. As a fellow Christian, she would have thought Mark would agree. However, now that she thought about it, when they'd shared their lunch break on Saturday, when it was time to say a blessing over their meal, he had let her lead in prayer. For the second time in only a few days, Mark didn't want to pray with her. Now she wondered if maybe something wasn't as it should have been. Traditionally, men automatically led with prayers, yet he hadn't.

She rested her hand on his forearm. "Is something wrong?"

He jerked his arm away as fast as if she had burned him with her touch. "Nothing is wrong. I just think we should get right to work. We have a lot to sort out and a lot to do."

"Which is why our first priority should be to pray about it. With God's guidance, everything will fall into place."

"Fall into place? You mean just like over the last few days? Uncle Jack's accident? Joe's heart attack? And me not knowing if I have a job to go back to? Life can't possibly fall more into place than that."

"You don't have to be so sarcastic."

"I'm not being sarcastic. I'm being realistic."

She wondered what had happened to Mark to make him so bitter, but this wasn't the time to ask. However, she couldn't *not* pray about something so important. Since Mark wasn't going to participate willingly, he left her no choice.

Once again, Chantelle reached out to touch Mark. This time, instead of just brushing his arm with her fingertips, she grabbed onto his sleeve and bowed her head quickly, trusting he wouldn't be rude and pull away when she had her eyes closed.

"Dear Lord, I ask that You watch over us and guide us today. Please help things go smoothly, and help us learn everything we need to know with the least amount of difficulty. Please put everyone's hearts at ease, and help us keep the business successful. I ask this in Jesus' name."

Chantelle paused, waiting for Mark to say something, but he remained silent. Very cautiously, she opened one eye just a little bit, just enough to look at Mark. He hadn't pulled away, but his eyes were closed and his brows were knotted as if he were deep in thought and at least following along with her spoken prayer. Even if he weren't speaking, Chantelle thought he was praying something, which made her feel better, but not great, about their supposed joint prayer for the diner and all that went with their temporary partnership.

Since they were still supposed to be praying, Chantelle said a silent prayer for Mark, that he could be healed of whatever was bothering him and that they could move forward with what they needed to do.

"Amen!" she finally chorused and released him.

"Amen," Mark mumbled.

Chantelle released his sleeve and walked to the counter leading into the kitchen. "I'm going to make coffee so we'll have a pot ready for when we open. What do you have to do first?"

Mark immediately jogged into the kitchen. "If nothing has changed in the last few years, then I should be baking muffins. There should be some batter already made in the refrigerator."

Going up on her tiptoes, Chantelle leaned over the counter and peeked as far as she could into the kitchen area. Mark opened the door to the walk-in refrigerator and disappeared inside. He was out of sight for exactly twenty seconds, then reappeared with a large plastic food-keeper.

"Apparently nothing has changed. It was in the first place I looked."

Without another word, he flipped on the oven to the right temperature and poured the batter into muffin tins.

The front door opened. Brittany walked in, waved a quick greeting to Chantelle, and headed down the stairs to the staff room. Brittany was barely out of sight when Kevin and Evelyn entered, also heading straight down the stairs. Mark nodded at Chantelle and followed them down, with Chantelle close behind.

As soon as Brittany, Kevin, and Evelyn saw Mark and Chantelle in the staff room, their eyebrows rose. Kevin very pointedly peered out the door, no doubt wondering why everyone had gathered in the small room and if Joe were also coming.

Mark cleared his throat and raised one palm in the air. "I'll get right to the point. Joe had a heart attack yesterday, and he's in the hospital." He paused during the collective gasp. "The prognosis so far looks good, but it's going to be awhile before he's back to normal and back to work. The same with my uncle Jack. Until they're back, Chantelle and I are going to oversee the diner. We want to assure you that it's business as usual until then." Mark paused to let what he said sink in.

Kevin was the first to respond. "What about your job? I thought you were supposed to be going back Sunday night."

"I'm staying until they come back to work." Mark looked past them as he spoke.

All three of them turned their heads toward Chantelle, waiting for her to confirm or deny everything Mark had said. She thought Mark had chosen his words well. Although it didn't feel very promising that he would be returning, neither of them really knew the status of Mark's job. Still, his boss hadn't actually said Mark was fired, so Chantelle couldn't help but hope that Mark's boss would consider holding the job for his return. She made a mental note to add that request, one of many things, to her rapidly growing prayer list.

"That's right. Brittany, you and I are going to take turns hostessing. I'll have to try and get the part-timers to fill in."

"Can we go to the hospital to see him? I guess he's not sharing a room with Jack."

"They're still only allowing immediate family as visitors for both of them."

Evelyn held her hands out. "I think we should all pray for Joe. Right now. Before anyone comes in."

Everyone murmured their agreement and shuffled into a circle. Chantelle noticed that Mark hesitated, but he did move with the others. However, a momentary flicker of panic crossed his face when Kevin on one side of him and Brittany on the other automatically reached over to hold his hands to complete the circle.

This time, since they were in the presence of others, and suspecting that Mark would not be quick to lead in a group prayer, Chantelle spoke out, asking for healing for both Uncle Joe and Jack. She didn't have time to continue to ask for the smooth operation of the diner while they were in the transition stage because the electronic beep sounded, announcing the first customers of the day had walked in.

Everyone muttered a quick "Amen," and the circle broke up.

"Okay, everybody!" Chantelle called out as cheerfully as she could. "Let's show the world what the employees at Joe's Diner are made of. Brittany, I think I'll take the first hosting so I can get used to it while it's quiet. I hope you don't mind."

"No, not at all."

Mark disappeared into the office with his laptop, and the three current staff members rushed off to their stations. Chantelle hurried to greet a group of men who looked and smelled like they'd been out camping and fishing all week-end. She seated them in one of the booths, where the vinyl seats could be easily wiped off, versus the padded fabric chairs, which would be difficult to wash.

Immediately following them, a group of businessmen entered. Brittany whispered in her ear that the same group came in every Monday and ordered the same thing—a nice healthy breakfast of fruit and muffins. Knowing Mark had already started baking the muffins, Chantelle felt relieved. She took care to seat the businessmen on the far side of the restaurant from the fishermen.

She had barely seated that group, when another large group of men entered. This group wore jeans, coveralls, and heavy, well-worn safety boots. She had seen this same group before, on Friday. Apparently, they came in two or three times a week, always ordering large, hungry-man bacon-and-egg breakfasts to get them started for a day of hard work outside.

Just like Friday, a steady stream of people kept everyone fairly busy. To streamline the operation, Chantelle seated all the customers and Brittany took all the orders. Together, they delivered all the food and checked up on the patrons.

Halfway through the morning, Mark took Chantelle aside. He glanced toward all the people who were enjoying their breakfasts, then back to Chantelle. "Everyone looks happy, and I haven't heard anything break so far. How's it going?"

Chantelle grinned. "Really well. Usually Uncle Joe does everything at the front and two servers are on duty, but lunchtime will be busier. Can you come up here and host for the heavy part of the lunch rush?"

"Sorry, but I have to leave for the airport. They called and said they located my luggage. We really need all of those records, and I could use my suitcase, too. I also have to go to the wholesaler right away because we're nearly out of a few things we need for the supper period. Kevin and I did our best to calculate what we're going to go through as to volume between now and Thursday without a database. Hopefully, I shouldn't have to make a second trip later in the week."

Chantelle forced herself to smile. She had only been a server for two days. Friday had been hectic even with Uncle Joe there. Today, she started to sag. She had been on her feet from the minute they walked in the door. The stress of learning the general operation of the restaurant without guidance or supervision, added to the lack of sleep the night before, left her feeling like a wrung-out dishrag.

All the enthusiasm she'd built as a reserve in preparation for the lunch rush dissolved in a puddle around her already aching feet. She had to force herself to smile. "That's good news."

Mark didn't smile back. "That's the only good news. I don't have a signature on file at the wholesaler, nor do they know who I am. I don't have a signed purchase order or a letter from Uncle Jack or Joe. That means, according to their policy, they don't recognize me as an authorized representative for the diner. They won't give me anything on credit. Being Monday morning, there's not enough money in the till to cover what we need, so I have to put the restaurant's order on my personal credit card. In fact, he told me that he's giving me special consideration to let me buy anything there at all, because I can't prove I work for the diner. A pay stub would have done it, but I don't have even that. According to regulations, they shouldn't let me buy anything at wholesale prices. He almost made me pay full retail."

Chantelle pressed both hands to her cheeks. "That's awful! What are we going to do? I don't think it would be good for either Uncle Joe or Jack if we started bringing in business problems already."

Mark narrowed one eye and rubbed his chin between his thumb and index finger. "I wonder if Aunt Susan or Ellen has a signature on file with the wholesaler. Neither of them work for the restaurant now, but maybe one of them did when they first started the business. I'll see what I can do to find either of them."

"Yes. You should go now. Hopefully, you'll be back in time for the change in shift. Rick and Sandra don't know what's happened yet."

Mark frowned and checked his watch. "I'll try. If I'm late, you'll do fine."

Without waiting for her to comment further, Mark disappeared out the front door, her keys in one hand and a long list in the other.

Chantelle didn't believe he didn't care if he were present when the next two staff members arrived. Rather, she suspected that he didn't want to be present because two more people whom he knew were their uncles' friends from church would probably want to pray for them.

Chantelle walked to the window to watch her car leave the parking lot. She didn't know what Mark's problem was, but she promised herself she would get to the bottom of it.

❧

A chorusing "amen!" echoed from the staff room while Mark made his way to the freezer laden with the first of many heavy boxes. Part of him felt sorry he'd missed being able to properly introduce himself to those he hadn't met yet. Another part of him felt relief that he arrived when he did. He no longer had to worry about getting stuck having to pray.

He almost stumbled at the direction of his thoughts. He knew Chantelle had figured out that he was avoiding praying, not only with people, but also privately. He didn't know how to explain to her that he didn't believe God listened to his prayers. Worse than that, everything he prayed for went even more wrong than when he didn't pray. He'd begun to wonder what God had against him.

For the first time in a long time, he'd broken down, and out of weakness, he'd prayed on the plane. He didn't know why he thought things might turn out better this time, because they hadn't. Everything his life touched became even worse, down to Joe's heart attack.

Now, not only did Mark not want to pray, he was afraid to.

As he propped the freezer door open with his foot, everyone hustled out of the staff room and upstairs, ready to begin the diner's next shift, leaving him completely alone in the basement. He quickly pushed the boxes of frozen meat inside the freezer and onto the proper shelves, then made his way to the stairs for the next trip.

Halfway up the stairs, he met Kevin on his way down.

Instead of moving aside, Kevin stopped, dead center. "I didn't know you were back. Want a little help putting all that stuff away?"

Mark opened his mouth to accept his offer, then hesitated. Kevin had finished his shift. Joe had been very specific about staff not working overtime. Mark recognized that Joe didn't want to incur too much extra expense. Even without paying overtime wages, the cost of the two extra salaries for himself and Chantelle, even at regular time, to replace both him and Jack would be costly. Joe also didn't want anyone to become overworked and overtired.

He looked at Kevin, who was still waiting for his answer. "That's okay. I know you're on your way out. Have a good evening, and I'll see you again tomorrow."

"Are you sure? I always pick my daughter up from school

when I get off, but I have time to make a couple of trips up."

Without waiting for Mark to agree or disagree, Kevin turned around and headed back upstairs, directly ahead of Mark.

Kevin made the predicted two trips down the stairs before he checked his watch and announced regretfully that he had to go. Mark thanked him, Kevin ran into the lunchroom to retrieve a book, and then scurried off, leaving Mark once again alone in the basement.

Mark stood without moving, his fists on his hips, and stared at the last spot he'd seen Kevin. Mark supposed he would find out when Kevin turned in his timesheet at the end of the week if the help was a favor or for fifteen minutes' overtime. If Mark had been back at the office, without a doubt, he would have been asked to pay overtime. With Kevin, Mark honestly didn't know, but he had a feeling Kevin was sacrificing his time simply as a favor. Such being the case, Mark didn't know how to react, as none of his staff at the accounting office would have stayed to help him unless there were money involved. Unlike him, they all disappeared the split second they were off the clock.

Knowing now what he didn't know then, Mark wondered if perhaps they had been the smart ones. He had allowed Sean to use him, and he'd received nothing in return for all his hard work except more work.

Mark shook his head to rid himself of his past mistakes and proceeded to unload the rest of the purchases himself. This was the time to move forward, once he figured out where forward was.

By the time he'd made a few more trips up and down the stairs and hoisted the last bag of pancake mix onto the shelf in the pantry, his back was screaming that he'd overdone it, making him even more grateful for Kevin's earlier help. It was almost torture to retrieve the last box from the car, which was the heavy box of documents.

Before he settled in to continue where he'd left off on

Saturday, Mark walked into the main dining area to inform Chantelle that he was back. Since she was busy with customers, he left her car keys on the counter beside the cash register and returned to the office.

He had barely sorted enough paperwork to start a few journal entries when Chantelle appeared in the doorway, jingling her car keys in the air before tucking them into her apron pocket.

"How are we going to work this, with one car between us? It's been over eight hours, but I can't leave. I think I'm going to be here until closing because I can't have Brad or Sandra hosting. That would leave only one server for the supper rush. It was bad enough with the two of us for lunch. I wouldn't want to do that again, and I certainly can't do that to anyone for the supper break. I don't mind giving you my car, but you'll have to come back after closing to get me."

Mark stopped typing and rested his palms on the edge of the keyboard. "I'm not going anywhere. I have too much to do. I'm also going to have to work in the kitchen during the supper break." He turned to study the staff's hours posted on the wall. "You've got Rick, who is full time, and then Allyson, who is a part-timer, in the kitchen for supper until closing. Two people would be okay for the evening, but not through the supper rush."

Chantelle nodded. "I hear Uncle Joe opened, worked a full day between the hosting and supervising, and Jack arrived sometime in the afternoon. He worked between the bookkeeping and the kitchen and stayed till closing."

"Are we going to do that?"

"I don't know. This should be an even swap of bodies, me for Uncle Joe and you for Jack, but it doesn't seem like we have enough people here. I even checked the week's schedule, and we have the right number of people. Somehow, it feels like we're always a person short. I don't know how they did it."

Mark nodded. Even though they had two different people, they were even with the body count on the schedule. Chantelle shouldn't have been having difficulty, yet there was no denying that she was.

To be fair, Joe had been running the restaurant for two decades, and Chantelle had stepped in with no advance preparation or training. He probably should have prayed that she would be able to figure everything out on her own, but he didn't dare.

He forced himself to smile politely. "I'm sure you'll figure it out, and you'll do fine."

"I don't know. I don't want to hire someone because Jack and Uncle Joe already have to pay you and me, which they didn't before. They're still going to need an income from this place, even though they're not here. But I really need another person serving or hosting. Can you tell if they pull in enough money to temporarily pay another extra salary?"

Mark fanned his arm over the mass of papers strewn all over the desktop, as well as a few stacks he didn't have enough room for, which had overflowed onto the floor. "Does it look like I know anything yet?"

She raised her eyebrows. "You don't have to be that way. I was just asking. If you want to go home, don't forget to get me at closing."

Before he could respond, she tossed her car keys into the middle of the desk, turned on her toes, and stomped off.

Mark shook his head and settled back into the chair. He winced at the twinge in his back as he twisted, then pressed both fists into the small of his back in an attempt to give himself some relief. The result of today's efforts made him grateful that he was, by profession, an accountant and not a truck driver.

He hadn't meant to be curt with Chantelle, but he had other things on his mind when she'd interrupted him. Being a career accountant meant he had a daunting task ahead of him.

After he caught up with the data entries, he also had to balance and reconcile everything. Then he had to make the system easy to maintain on a daily basis.

What had probably made him less than patient was that Chantelle hadn't been the only one to wonder if the diner could support the extra salaries. From what he'd seen so far, he didn't think it could. He hadn't told Chantelle, but he'd given her a raise in pay to offset the difference between serving and hosting, because now she would no longer be in a position to collect tips, which would have been a substantial component of her income. Mark wanted to do the fair thing, which was also what his uncle would have done.

Knowing what he knew of the way his uncle and Joe conducted their business, Mark was almost afraid to continue. By experience, he'd seen that Ma-and-Pa–run proprietorships usually didn't profit as well as ventures that were strictly "business." The cold, hard facts of life proved over and over that most of the time, nice guys really did finish last.

Even if Uncle Jack and Joe could take a hard line with the business, he still didn't know how the business would fare with the drain of two additional and unexpected salaries. Back in his college days, he'd thought the diner had done well, but that was through the eyes of inexperience. Besides, at the time, he hadn't been given the opportunity to audit the financial records. All he'd seen was what his uncle had wanted him to see.

A few days ago, he had given everything only a cursory audit due to time constraints. Then, paying extra salaries hadn't been an issue. Now he had to look at the paperwork in a different light, which was managing it rather than just entering and balancing. Having seen too much struggling by businesses when unexpected disasters happened, the real question in his mind was if paying himself and Chantelle fair salaries would be too much and drive the business under.

Another thing Chantelle hadn't considered was medical

expenses. If either or both of their uncles didn't have good medical plans or enough saved, the money would have to come from somewhere. That somewhere could only be the restaurant, their only source of investment.

Mark sighed as he reached for the first stack of paper, which was the pile of purchase orders to be entered. Until he could get control of it, every second he wasn't urgently needed in the kitchen would be spent searching for answers in the jumble before him.

Just as he touched the first order in the pile, Chantelle's boisterous laughter echoed into the small office.

Mark gritted his teeth. Every so often, she irritated him to no end, and this was one of those times. While he was slaving away in the office all by himself, she was in the middle of the action, having fun. The woman had no concept of what it took to run a business successfully.

And, he vowed to himself, in spite of Chantelle, he was going to do everything he had to do to make this one successful.

Mark rose and closed the office door, just short of slamming it. As he sat down, a shot of pain seared through his abdomen. His head swam. Mark sucked in a deep breath and pressed his fist into his solar plexus until it subsided. He didn't know which one would be the final touch to drive him over the edge to a full-fledged ulcer—the latest calamity that had been cast into his lap or Chantelle.

nine

Chantelle seated a couple of people who had just made the most awful joke. She forced herself to smile as she bid her leave, even though it almost hurt.

She didn't know if it was because she was so tired or if it was because of all the stress of the day. To the customers, she could be nice, but to Mark, she'd almost said something she surely would have regretted.

So far, she considered herself to have been patient and understanding with Mark. He had been thrust into a new situation very unexpectedly, even more so than she had. He'd been uprooted from his job and his home. The only bright side was, instead of living alone, he was staying with his parents, who fed him and probably didn't expect him to do any of the housework while he was there—at least not yet.

Just as she reached the counter leading to the kitchen, she heard the office door close with an abrupt bang.

Chantelle gritted her teeth. She knew what he was thinking, and it hurt.

It was obvious that Mark didn't think much of her abilities as a waitress. Despite the fact that he was right and that she didn't particularly like waitressing, it still stung. He hadn't said anything directly, but Chantelle wasn't stupid. She could see the underlying thread of impatience in him. She certainly heard the sarcasm in his voice. She may not be very good, but she was doing the job to the best of her obviously limited abilities. All she wanted was to hear that there was hope. That they really could pull together and run the diner. . .and most of all, that tomorrow things would be easier.

He hadn't given her the chance.

"Chantelle? Table twenty-two is asking if we have soy burgers. Do we?"

Chantelle spun around to face Sandra. Her first management question and she didn't know the answer. But since she didn't know, she had to assume the answer was no.

"Tell them we're sorry, we don't have anything not on the menu. If they don't want beef, suggest a chicken burger; if they're looking for a diet or meatless meal, suggest a fresh garden salad. I know that we do have some kind of fat-free dressing. I just don't know what flavor it is."

Sandra smiled and nodded. "Great. I'll do that."

Chantelle made a mental note to study the menu and options better.

She didn't want to start doubting herself, but she wondered what Uncle Joe would have told her to say. Then, since she didn't have Uncle Joe to ask, she wondered what Mark would have said.

Chantelle shook her head. Mark wasn't here. He was in the office with the door closed, shut away from everything and everybody, having a stress attack all by himself.

All she wanted was a little bit of encouragement from him. She would readily have done the same for him if it looked like he needed it. Right now, she thought he did. However, instead of making himself accessible, he pushed everyone away, including her.

Last night, though, he certainly hadn't pushed her away. She'd been the one to push him away. Now she realized that she'd made a mistake. If they were going to be partners, they had to at least be friends. Friends could indeed share a hug. However, friends shouldn't be sharing a kiss.

Chantelle covered her face with her hands. They hadn't exactly shared a kiss. All he'd done was kiss the top of her head. Or maybe he hadn't. Maybe she'd imagined it. Today she was sure that kissing her was the furthest thing from his mind. His impatience with her had been more than clear. She had no idea what he'd been thinking last night; but today, she had a feeling that she didn't want to know.

Chantelle straightened at the sound of the bell announcing the arrival of more customers. She pasted on a smile, showed them to a table, gave them menus, and returned to the front.

For her first day at hostessing, except for being so tired, she thought she might like the job. She liked dealing with a variety of people. Most of all, she found she much preferred taking their money than serving the food.

Mark, on the other hand, didn't enjoy working with people, even though she knew he was a manager at his real job. He seemed to prefer to spend his day alone in the office with his computer or in the kitchen, working with only two or three other people.

Still, she had to be fair. For now, Mark did have to shoulder the bulk of responsibility for making the restaurant run smoothly. Until he finished entering all of his uncle's data into the computer, they were operating blind—even down to the stock they needed from day to day. Without the schedule on the wall in the staff room, she wouldn't have known who was working or what times they were supposed to show up. Until Mark finished inputting countless pieces of paper and doing whatever it was accountants did, they had to operate on pure grace, hoping and praying that all went as it was supposed to.

A grumble from Chantelle's stomach hit her at the same time as a wave of nausea surged through her. Slowly, supporting herself by resting one hand on the edge of the empty table closest to the front counter, she lowered herself to sit down. For the first time that day, she checked her watch. She'd known when two-thirty had come because the two other full-time people had arrived, and the early starters had gone home. But she hadn't thought about the time other than a marker in the day because of the change of staff. It was now four-thirty, and Chantelle just realized that she had not yet stopped for a break. That also meant she hadn't eaten anything since five-thirty that morning, when she'd gobbled down a couple of pieces of toast and a glass of juice on her way out the door to pick up Mark.

She needed something to eat, and she probably needed to lie down for a minute.

But she couldn't leave the front because that would leave Sandra alone.

What would Uncle Joe do?

Uncle Joe would check on Mark, because he probably hadn't eaten or had a break, either.

But at least Mark had been sitting down for most of the day.

Chantelle sucked in a deep breath and stood. She walked in a very determined straight line to the kitchen, trying to ignore the spinning in her head.

"Excuse me, Rick? Can you give me a quick order of fries on the side? They're for me. I need something to nibble on. Can you tell me if Mark has had anything to eat since you've come in?"

Rick nodded. "Yes, Mark took a number six back into Jack's office about half an hour ago. I also saw him help himself to a muffin earlier."

Chantelle sighed. Apparently, Mark was better able to take care of himself than she was. However, Mark didn't have to worry about being unable to leave his post for longer than it took to make a quick run to the washroom. And, she certainly couldn't be eating in front of customers as they walked in the door, where he was free to eat at the desk.

"Make that a number six for me, too, then. Call me when it's ready. I'll be right back." She turned to Sandra, pointed to the office, then to her watch, and held up two fingers. "Two minutes." When Sandra acknowledged her, Chantelle walked to the office.

She stood at the door, inhaled deeply, then gave the door a sharp knock. However, the door hadn't been shut all the way.

The door whooshed open, hitting the wall behind Mark as he worked. At the bang, Mark jumped, knocking a few papers from beside his laptop onto the floor.

Chantelle didn't give him a chance to speak. "I know you're busy, but we need to talk."

He ran his fingers through his hair, then bent to pick what he had dropped. "You could have knocked."

"Sorry. I meant to. I need you to replace me at the front. I need a break."

He glanced at his wristwatch. "Can't it wait? The other two staff members will be arriving in about half an hour."

"That's because half an hour will be the start of the supper rush, and I haven't even had lunch."

Mark sprang to his feet. "No lunch? Are you telling me you haven't had a break yet?" His brows knotted. "We've been here eleven hours. Are you crazy?"

Chantelle planted her fists on her hips. "Apparently."

He leaned toward his laptop and hit save. "Go take your break. In fact, you should go home. Don't worry about me at closing. I'll take a cab. Just give me your key, and I'll lock up."

She waved one hand in the air. The motion of her own hand almost sent her off balance. Chantelle shuffled her feet to steady herself. "I'm not going home. Who is going to host at the front for the rest of the night? Certainly not you."

"I beg your pardon? You just asked me to look after the front for you a few minutes ago."

"That's different. I'm fully prepared to work a few long days until we get everything figured out around here. All I need is for someone to watch things while I eat and take a short break, then I can go back to the front. And you shouldn't talk about needing a break and going home. You've had your face buried in that computer most of the day. How are you able to concentrate?"

He crossed his arms over his chest. "I've put in longer days than this many times. I'm doing just fine. You, on the other hand, look a bit pale."

Chantelle wanted to assure him that she was fine, but the room started to spin, and suddenly she felt warm. She raised her fingers and pressed them to her temples. "I think maybe I should sit down."

She started to walk in the direction of the chair. At her second step, her legs wobbled and the room began to go dark. One knee gave out. She felt herself falling, and there was nothing she could do about it.

Somewhere in the distance, she heard her name being called. A strong arm wrapped around her waist, supporting her while some strength came back into her legs. Automatically, she reached out and hung on to a pair of wide shoulders. Slowly, Mark's face came into focus.

Mark's voice came out in a low rumble. "What's wrong? Are you okay?"

All the spinning had stopped, but Chantelle struggled to find her voice. When she could speak, it came out barely above a squeak. "I'm sorry. This has happened before. I should know better than to go so long without eating. I'll be fine."

Before she had a chance to let go and back up, Mark's mouth was on hers. He kissed her hard and quick. Then, as quickly as he kissed her, it was over.

He didn't let her go as he spoke. His voice came out all thick and rumbly. "You scared me."

Her brain misfired in a million directions. She almost had formed a coherent thought she could turn into a sentence when a male voice sounded, but this time Mark's mouth wasn't moving.

"Your lunch is ready, Chantelle, and. . ." The voice trailed off.

Mark turned his head in the direction of the doorway, so Chantelle did, too.

Rick stood in the doorway, his mouth hanging open. He blinked a few times in rapid succession, and his face turned beet red. "Sorry. I didn't mean to interrupt. The door was open. Mark, you have a call on line two. It sounds like Ellen."

As quickly as Rick appeared, he disappeared.

In that same split second, Mark released her and stepped back.

Chantelle broke out into a cold sweat. "I think I'd better go eat my lunch and get back to the front," she mumbled. In a split second, she turned and hustled to the kitchen counter as quickly as she could without looking like she was running. She kept her head fixed straight ahead so she wouldn't catch Rick's eyes. As she picked up her lunch, she muttered a quick "thank you," then hurried downstairs to the staff room.

With all the conflicting thoughts roaring through her head, Chantelle had to force herself to focus on a short prayer of thanks for her meal before she started eating.

If the same thing had happened fifty years ago, she would have slapped Mark's face.

But it wasn't fifty years ago.

And she didn't want to slap his face.

Chantelle shoveled four fries into her mouth at once and gulped them down before she'd really chewed them properly.

Mark had kissed her. But she didn't really like him. Or did she? The way he made such snap decisions and tended to be bossy annoyed her. At the same time, she also admired his leadership ability, which was probably the same trait in a different application. While she knew that she was a "people person," Mark tended to separate himself from people in general. But he wasn't antisocial; he got along well with everyone he came in contact with. He just tended to be quiet in a crowd, unlike herself. He'd been quite disturbed after Uncle Joe's heart attack, and he'd given up his job to stay and help. Deep down, he really was a caring person.

If she closed her eyes and thought of Mark, the first picture to appear was of him performing CPR on Uncle Joe. Mark had saved Uncle Joe's life. If ever there was a case of admiration, even hero-worship, that was it.

Chantelle bit into her burger, taking in so much, she almost had to chew with her mouth open.

Admiring Mark wasn't the same as liking him. In order to like someone, you had to know them, and she really didn't know him that well. Most important, whether she liked him or not, despite whatever potential they had for a relationship, they both knew he was leaving as soon as their uncles returned to work.

She'd said it before, but she reminded herself again. She refused to set herself up for a potential heartbreak. He was leaving; therefore, nothing would be starting, no matter how she felt about him.

She gobbled down the hamburger and fries in record time. Not wanting to lie down with a full stomach, Chantelle ran up the stairs and returned to the front counter. She took a gentleman's money while Mark seated an older couple.

On his return trip to the front counter, Mark showed no signs of awkwardness or regret. In fact, she didn't see signs of anything, not even that he was glad to see her. All he did was check his wristwatch. "Are you back already? You were only gone ten minutes. That's not long enough for a break."

"And I suppose you took a break? Rick told me that you ate in the office while you were working."

"I'm busy, Chantelle. I ate at my desk, but it was still a break. If we were at S&B, I'd insist you take your full lunch break. Besides, I didn't almost pass out."

"We're not at S&B, so those rules don't apply. I could say the same thing to you. You should be taking your full break, and you're not supposed to be working overtime."

He grinned. "You know I would just take everything to my parents' house and work on it there, except that here I have everything on hand if I require more information. Besides, for awhile, working only eight hours a day isn't an option. I have to get this done. The smooth operation of the diner depends on this information."

She couldn't argue with him, so she decided to change the subject. "What did Aunt Ellen want?"

Mark sighed. "Joe has been asking for us. From five o'clock till closing we'll have two people each in the kitchen and serving, besides ourselves. After the supper rush is over, we'll have to go to the hospital. I don't know what we're going to tell him. We should also go see Uncle Jack. I think they're allowing him to have visitors now."

"We can tell both of them that everything is going just fine and that you're still working on catching up."

"I guess."

Chantelle checked her wristwatch, then started counting on her fingers. "I think the best time to leave would be about eight-fifteen. Would that work for you?"

He nodded and was gone so fast Chantelle barely had time to blink. She seated only a few more groups when Allyson and Brad arrived. Unable to leave her post with the supper rush starting, Chantelle did her best to explain what happened and sent them on their way to get ready.

With both Sandra and Brad serving, the supper rush went much more smoothly than the lunch rush. Having Allyson in the kitchen gave them the ideal number, according to Uncle Joe, for a restaurant this size.

Smooth operations aside, by the time eight-fifteen rolled around and Mark appeared, she felt like she was ready to drop. Chantelle thought that if she had to smile nicely at one more pair of strangers, she would surely die.

Mark held the door open for her as they walked outside and jingled her keys in the air. "Want me to drive?"

Normally, Chantelle would have argued. It was her car, and while she was in it, she drove it.

"Sure," she mumbled and walked directly to the passenger door, waiting for him to unlock it.

During the trip to the hospital, Chantelle stretched out her tired legs and her aching feet, leaned her head back, and closed her eyes. What she really wanted to do was take off her shoes; but she knew that if she took them off, she'd never get them back on.

"You must be exhausted. I guess I'm lucky because, even though it's been a long day, I've been sitting most of the time."

Chantelle didn't bother to reply.

"Are you sure we're doing the right thing leaving? I couldn't believe my eyes when Allyson walked in. I don't think she's more than twenty years old. And the same with the boy who is serving. Did you put anyone officially in charge?"

"They're adults. They'll be fine," she mumbled, fighting to keep her eyes open. "Besides, I gave them your cell number."

"I don't know. Rick and Sandra both appear to be in their early twenties, but Allyson and Brad are students, working evenings while going to school."

Chantelle let her eyes drift shut. "Not school. College. You did the same thing. You were trustworthy, weren't you?"

"That's different."

"No, it's not. The only difference is that you're Jack's relative. All four of them are Jack and Uncle Joe's Christian brothers and sisters. Jack and Uncle Joe trust them, and that's all we need to know."

"I guess I can't argue, can I?"

Chantelle didn't answer. Mark remained silent, which was both good and bad. Good, because she wasn't sure she wanted to talk to him until she sorted out what happened earlier, but bad, because she could feel herself falling asleep, and she couldn't do anything about it.

The car came to a stop. "Chantelle? Are you sleeping?"

Slowly, she opened her eyes. "Almost. Sorry. I didn't mean to be rude."

"Don't worry about it. Before we go in, we should talk about what to tell Joe and Uncle Jack. I'm not finished entering and reconciling everything yet. So far, things look borderline, but okay. Still, I don't think the diner can pay another additional full-time salary like you want. Remember, the restaurant still has to pay Uncle Jack and Joe even though they're not there."

Chantelle felt herself sag. "I don't know if I find that too encouraging, but I suppose it's better than what you could have said. Let's go."

ten

Mark rolled over and pulled the blanket up to his chin. Despite being thoroughly exhausted, he couldn't sleep.

Every time he closed his eyes, he saw different images of Chantelle. Of her smiling. Or how she pressed her fists into her back when she thought he wasn't watching. How she constantly fiddled with those silly clips in her hair.

The image most clear in his mind was of her expression after he kissed her. Her eyes were closed, her lips slightly parted. He had seriously thought of kissing her again, right this time, when Rick barged in.

Mark squeezed his eyes shut, but it didn't help. The total blackness only made his memories more vivid.

He tried to make sense of what was happening. He couldn't.

Just as Chantelle started to fall, the memory of Joe collapsing at the airport flashed through his mind. Unlike Joe, Mark had managed to catch Chantelle before she hit the floor. He still didn't know why he had kissed her. Yet, at the time, he couldn't *not* kiss Chantelle. Even though it wasn't likely that Chantelle could also be having a heart attack, the thought of something being seriously wrong made his stomach churn. He should have been angry with her that she'd caused the problem herself by not eating for so long, especially after she admitted it had happened before. Yet, he couldn't be angry.

The woman was going to drive him insane.

The way Chantelle disappeared when Rick returned to the kitchen told Mark he'd stepped past her boundaries when he'd kissed her. She'd already hugged him, so if he'd just hugged her and not kissed her, she likely would have stayed. But he'd gone further than that. He'd kissed her, and he shouldn't have. They didn't know each other well enough for that. He wasn't even sure he liked her that much. At times, she drove him crazy with her overexuberance and Pollyanna attitude.

But the woman had spunk. Once she set her mind to doing something, she did it, no matter what.

She also had guts. Not many people stood up to him, and he was seldom challenged. When he was, he seldom lost. He had a feeling that Chantelle not only would hold her ground against him, occasionally she might even win.

Mark found himself grinning at the possibilities.

He'd experienced his first taste of how skillfully she could steer a conversation while at the hospital. Uncle Jack was still confined to bed, being only a few days after surgery; but Joe convinced a nurse to put him in a wheelchair and push him into Uncle Jack's room so they could all talk together. Mark did his best to assure them that even though he hadn't yet managed to catch up on all the financial records, it didn't look like irreparable damage had been done, except for the computer itself.

Strangely, when he said he was staying, Uncle Jack hadn't seemed all that surprised. It had been Joe who had asked how Mark had managed to get so much time off with no notice. Mark couldn't think of a reply that wouldn't make them feel bad, but Chantelle jumped into the conversation at that point. She revealed a select bit of information from his phone conversation with Sean, then changed the subject so fast neither of them realized they were no longer talking strictly business. Before they knew it, she was telling slightly exaggerated stories of amusing things that happened at the diner that day. She actually had Joe laughing until the nurse came in and asked them to leave because she was causing a disturbance.

Uncle Jack and Joe were both happy to hear that he had partnered with Chantelle to run the diner until their return. He still didn't know if it would work. All he could do was his best.

Mark rolled over and forced himself to keep his eyes closed. Five-thirty would come far too quickly. Tomorrow would be another day of arduous, long hours.

And another day of working with Chantelle.

❧

"Good morning. Did you sleep well?" Chantelle smiled at him, her bright, cheerful grin almost making him forget how little sleep he really did get.

"Once I was out, I slept like a log. And you?"

"I feel much better than yesterday. Now buckle up your seatbelt. We're on our way."

Mark studied Chantelle as she drove. For once, she didn't talk. Any other day, he would have appreciated the silence. This time, though, they were in for another long day, and there were things that needed to be said.

As a manager, he knew from experience that short stretches of blitzing a large workload could produce exceptional results. However, past a certain point, too much overwork became counterproductive. He knew as much by falling into the same pit too many times himself. Still, even if he didn't take the breaks he knew he should, he always made sure his staff took their breaks. He'd certainly never had an employee faint on him before.

Not that she was an employee, but Chantelle seemed unable to recognize her own danger signs, nor did she know how to pace herself. Therefore, Mark decided to save Chantelle from herself.

"I was thinking about yesterday. We have to make sure the same thing doesn't happen again."

Her face paled. "Yesterday?"

"Yes. Yesterday. You know, when—"

"I know what happened yesterday."

Mark knotted his brows at her sharp tone, but continued anyway. "Good. Then I think you'll agree that we should take our breaks. We'll schedule them to coincide with nonpeak periods. Of course, I don't need to be relieved; but up at the front, you do. You can have one of the servers relieve you or I can. We don't want any of the servers pushing themselves too hard by hosting and serving at the same time. It's up to you to make sure the servers take their scheduled breaks, and I'll make sure the cooks take theirs."

"That's what this is all about? Coffee breaks?"

"Well. . .yes. . ."

Before he could comment further, she quickly agreed, then changed the subject without a breath in between and started talking nonstop.

Mark turned to the window so she wouldn't see him grinning. He had already noticed that Chantelle talked even more than usual when she was nervous or wanted to distract someone. He could understand her embarrassment. If he had fainted at work, he would be embarrassed, too. He, however, would have simply apologized and let it go.

As soon as they arrived at the diner, Mark made a quick trip to the kitchen to put the morning muffins in the oven, then hastened to the office and immediately resumed re-entering the data. The alarm on his wristwatch went off at exactly the right time to remind him to tell Chantelle to take her break.

At first, she protested; but as soon as he mentioned the previous day's events, she fell silent and did as she was told. She returned precisely fifteen minutes later, the first time she'd been on time for anything since he met her.

Before he could get too smug about his little victory, Chantelle made an appearance at the office door when he was right in the middle of an important transaction. Her voice was almost like an echo of his own, reminding him to put his work down and go downstairs into the staff room for his break. He tried to tell her that he was too busy and didn't need the break, but she wouldn't listen. For someone who had to write down every component of an order in longhand, she threw his own words back at him with the accuracy of a tape recorder. He ended up taking that break and all his others when she asked, just so he wouldn't have to listen to her. The worst part was that every time he saw her, she winked at him and pointed to her watch.

Having to eat his own words wouldn't have been so bad if she hadn't been gloating about it.

By the end of the day, he was so angry with her he could barely look at her. He wasn't used to taking breaks every two hours, and he certainly wasn't used to being banished to the staff room for a full half-hour twice a day, because she made him take the full break for dinner, too. His only consolation was that she was taking all her breaks, all of the proper duration, as well.

However, because of Chantelle, it was taking longer than anticipated to re-enter the lost data. At this rate, despite being at the diner from opening until closing, Mark had a bad feeling he wouldn't be finished until sometime on Saturday.

On the drive home, he tried to figure out some way to convince Chantelle to take her breaks while he worked through his; but every time he brought the conversation around to break time, she changed the subject.

When they arrived at his parents' house, she bade him a friendly farewell. He got out, being careful to push the door hard enough to close it, but at the same time trying not to slam it too hard—a near impossibility. On the third try, it finally closed properly; but just as it caught, he thought of one more argument to win his case on the coffee break issue. He tapped on the hood of the car to get her attention so she wouldn't run him over and then jogged around the front to stand beside her door.

He waited while she struggled with the handle to open the window, but it only opened two inches and stuck.

Mark tapped his foot, not caring if he looked as impatient as he felt. Every extra minute she took to fool around with the window took a minute out of his sleep time and hers, something neither of them would be getting enough of that night or for many nights to come. It was already nearly eleven P.M. The countdown to getting up at five-thirty A.M. had already begun, and he still wasn't even in the house, never mind in bed.

"Just get out of the car already," he snapped.

She froze, her eyes widened, and she looked up at him. Very slowly, she exited the car and stood in front of him.

Her voice came out as softly as a whisper on the wind. "Yes?"

All Mark's anger melted. At the diner when they were both running around trying to keep up with the latest crisis of the hour, energy levels were piqued and adrenaline levels were high. It was easy for him to stay pumped. Now, here, when they were so tired he didn't know how they both could stand, everything came more into perspective.

Chantelle wasn't his enemy. They were both striving toward a common goal, which was the success of the diner. The little coffee-break battle they carried through the entire day, much to the amusement of all the employees, was meant to be for the good of each other. It had worked. They had both worked fifteen-hour days, and neither of them had made any mistakes or done anything wrong, except for one little piece of pie that went flying off a plate when Chantelle turned around too fast.

He didn't want to fight with Chantelle. She was his friend.

"Come here." He extended his arms, inviting her closer.

Much to his relief, Chantelle smiled and accepted his offer. She snuggled up to him, wrapped her arms around his back, and he did the same to her. Mark buried his face into the top of her head, being careful not to hit his nose on any of the plastic clips that hadn't fallen out.

Her hair didn't smell like apple shampoo this time. In fact, after a long day at the diner, she smelled a little like greasy French fries. Still, he couldn't think of anyplace else he'd rather be.

"It's been a long day, but we did great," he muttered.

Briefly, she gave him a small squeeze, then released him, so he did the same.

"Good night, Mark," she said softly. She shuffled back into the car and drove away.

Mark stood at the curb, smiling, watching the car until the taillights disappeared around the corner.

He couldn't kiss her; but if every night they parted with a hug, then all would be well with his soul.

Still, hugs or not, it was going to be a long week.

&

Mark opened one eye and smacked at his wristwatch on the night table to get the sound to stop. As his head cleared, he realized it wasn't his alarm that was beeping. It was the electronic tone of his cell phone, ringing from his pants pocket, on the other side of the bedroom.

He flung the blankets aside, barely managing not to trip when his bare feet touched the cold hardwood floor. Grumbling every step of the way, he stumbled across the room and groped at the lump that was his pants until he found his cell phone.

"Hi, Mark! I was wondering what time you wanted me to pick you up?"

"Chantelle?" he mumbled, then shook his head to wake himself up enough to carry on a conversation. He shuffled back across the room and picked up his wristwatch. He squinted and held the watch up to his face, struggling to focus on the numbers without his contacts in. The time was nine A.M. "I'm sorry, I must have overslept. I didn't hear the doorbell. Are you at the diner?"

"No, Silly. It's Sunday!" she chorused in the most annoying little singsong voice he'd ever heard. "I was just calling to see what time you wanted me to pick you up for church!"

"Church? I was going to sleep in."

"No, no, nooo-oh. . . ," she sang into the phone, making

Mark wince. "You already have slept in. The service starts at ten. I'll be there at nine-forty. See you later!"

A click sounded in his ear.

"I thought you were going to ask," he grumbled to the dial tone, then flipped the unit closed.

He crossed the room to get his bathrobe out of the closet so he could take a shower, but stopped before he opened the door. He looked at himself in the mirrored bifold door. Even without his contacts, he didn't like what he saw.

He'd put in countless long hours over the years, but it had never shown on him before, at least not like this. He was barely awake, and already dark circles shadowed his eyes. His skin seemed too pale, not only because he was spending the bulk of the summer indoors.

Mark stiffened and straightened his posture, but he still looked like a scruffy mess. Aside from not having shaved yet and added to the rude awakening, his hair stood out in clumps. It reminded him that he couldn't remember when he last had time to get a haircut.

He stood, unmoving, staring at his pathetic reflection. The last week had been the worst alleged vacation of his life. He couldn't remember ever being so tired, even though last night was the most sleep he'd gotten all week because the diner opened half an hour later on Saturday than on the weekdays. Still, by the time they'd cleaned up and locked the doors, Chantelle had dropped him off at eleven P.M. For the first time in his life, he'd gone from the front door straight into the bedroom, leaving his clothes in a trail across the floor as he fell into bed.

The good part of the week, though, was that he finally finished everything he needed to do. Everything had been re-entered and reconciled, including an accompanying database. Both he and Chantelle now had signing authority at the bank, and he'd given everyone their paychecks on time. All he had left to do was network the computer to the cash register to tally the orders as they were charged to the customers. Then, once a day, he needed to enter only whatever had been spilled or disposed of at the close of business. In the tap of one keystroke, the computer would generate the order for the following week. From now on, nothing would be left to guesswork or to chance.

On Monday, they could start afresh with a new schedule having fewer hours per day for both of them. That afternoon, he was going to lease a car, which would gain him some independence.

If only he could get one good night's sleep, life would again be good.

After putting in his contacts, he poked his head out the bathroom door. "Mom? Dad?"

Only silence answered him. He padded barefoot into the kitchen, where he found a note on the table. He sat on a stool at the kitchen counter to read the note.

Hi Mark,
   We went to church, but you were sleeping so soundly, we decided to leave you alone. We're probably going out for lunch with friends, so we'll see you at suppertime.

Love,
Mom and Dad

Mark sighed and squeezed his eyes shut. His parents understood him. Chantelle on the other hand. . . That was another story.

He sighed again and slouched back down the hallway to the bathroom to run the water for his shower. He doubted she would be on time, but he refused to let her bad habits affect him. He would be ready on time even if she wasn't.

Soon, Mark felt human again. This time, when he stood in front of the mirror, shaved, refreshed, and able to focus properly, he was more satisfied with himself. However, when he opened the closet door, his mood again fell to discouragement.

Working six days a week from sunrise to well after sunset, he hadn't had time to go shopping. All he had with him was the contents of his one suitcase, which was only meant for one weekend. His mother, bless her soul, had felt sorry for him and bought him one additional change of clothes, then done laundry midweek to let the three outfits he had last him. However, today all that hung in the closet was one shirt, one pair of pants, and a tie belonging to his father—the same thing he'd worn to church last week.

He ran his hand down his face. Tomorrow, he would courier the key to his apartment and ask a friend to pack up and ship some things to him. He also needed to make arrangements to store his car somewhere and see if he could sublet his apartment rather than paying rent and having it vacant.

He groaned out loud as he thought of the contents of his refrigerator, which he hadn't even looked at when he got home from work the Friday he left. He had expected to be back two days later, not even enough time to worry about the milk going sour. But after over a week. . .

Rather than stand in one spot feeling sorry for himself, Mark dressed, made a quick breakfast, and was ready to go when Chantelle arrived, to his surprise, on time.

Instead of going to their uncles' church, she took him to her own, where she felt more comfortable.

She seemed to know everyone there, from infants to the elderly. By the time they made it to the sanctuary and were seated, he'd been introduced to so many people, he knew he would never remember a single one of them, except for Tyler, the teen with the blue spikes in his hair.

He turned to Chantelle, meaning to ask what time the service ended, but his words caught in his throat. He didn't know why he hadn't noticed earlier, but Chantelle looked as bad as he felt. She wore only a bare hint of lipstick and eye shadow, which emphasized the lack of any attempt to hide the dark circles under her eyes. Even her unruly hair had lost its bounce. Although she never seemed to lose that effervescent cheerfulness, her eyes seemed dull, giving away how the long hours had more than caught up with her.

To cut her driving time and allow her more sleep, Mark made a mental note that leasing a car would definitely come before buying more clothes.

The lights dimmed, and the service began. He found he knew some of the worship songs. Although not having attended his own church much in the last year, he didn't know some of the choruses that appeared to be fairly new to Chantelle's congregation.

As they sat to hear the sermon, Chantelle pulled a small-print full-version mini-sized Bible out of her purse. When she noticed him squinting to read it, she handed it to him. Not that he particularly wanted to read it, but out of politeness, he was now obligated to follow along, holding it to the side so both of them could share. The print was so small, his eyes burned with the strain to read, forcing him to hold it closer than he normally liked to position his reading material. While the pastor read a very long passage, he felt Chantelle lean her shoulder against his, telling him that she, too, felt the strain of tired eyes and needed it closer.

Because the pastor often referred to verses within the text, Mark continued to hold the Bible up during the sermon.

Quite frankly, Mark found the message quite ordinary and the pastor uninspiring. Besides, he figured there was nothing God had to say to him. Instead of paying attention, Mark read past the section the pastor was preaching on, hoping no one would notice as he turned the page. Actually, since he probably would never be back there, Mark didn't really care if anyone noticed. They would never see him again. The only one he had to worry about was Chantelle, because he had to see her every single day for the next four months. If there were one thing he had learned about her, it was that once she got an idea stuck in her head, nothing in the universe could change it, not even good old common sense and reasoned logic.

As he continued to read the story of Daniel, he noticed that Chantelle hadn't stopped leaning on him.

He smiled to himself, wondering if she were as bored as he was and was also reading with him. Just before he turned the page again, he cocked his head slightly to ask if she were ready for him to flip the page. However, instead of reading, her eyes were closed. He moved slightly to look at her better. With the slight movement, her head bobbed, then flopped to the side, resting on his shoulder.

Mark forced himself to keep a straight face. Obviously, he wasn't the only person less than enamored with the pastor's monologue.

However, sitting in church with Chantelle leaning on him and sleeping put him in a quandary. It was church, after all. It seemed disrespectful to sleep through the pastor's message, despite the fact that he knew how tired she was.

Still, he didn't know if he wanted to wake her up. If he poked her, he would be taking the chance that she would be startled and jump or, worse, scream, which he wouldn't put past her.

Therefore, as long as she didn't snore, Mark decided to let her sleep.

Instead of reading, Mark found himself staring blankly, the words blurring on the page in front of him while the pastor's voice droned on. The warmth of Chantelle on his shoulder distracted him, drawing all his thoughts to her instead of what was going on around him.

He knew how exhausted he felt—it was all he could do to keep his own eyes open. More than that, he was accustomed to unreasonable hours of work and she wasn't. Plus, over the past week, he'd spent the majority of his time as he usually did, sitting down with his face glued to a computer. Chantelle, on the other hand, had spent most of the time on her feet and walking around, maintaining a cheerful presentation as she dealt with customers from opening until closing.

He specifically remembered on Saturday night, she'd traded duties with one of the servers for an hour. All Mark could see were dollar signs flitting through his mind as he added up the possibilities of what she could drop, spill, or break. But, if she wanted a change in her routine, he would do his best to push aside his worries. Putting in the long days as they had been doing all week, he at least had had the opportunity to change between accounting and cooking. He wanted to be fair to allow Chantelle some variety, although admittedly there wasn't much difference that he could see between serving and hosting.

She'd done fine until just before closing, when he came out of the office to tell her that he'd finally finished compiling the database.

It all happened in the blink of an eye. As he started to speak, she turned her head. Not watching where she was going, she walked into the corner of one of the tables. She hadn't fallen down, but everything on the tray she'd been carrying went flying and crashed to the floor. He couldn't bear to see the mess and all the broken dishes, so he'd closed his eyes, hoping everything was a cruel figment of his imagination.

Then he heard her sniffle. When he opened his eyes, everyone in the area was looking down at the mess, but he looked at Chantelle. Tears shimmered in her eyes as she stood, immobile, pressing both hands into her thigh at the spot she'd impacted with the table.

She'd hurt herself. At the time, she'd just cleaned off a couple of tables and her tray was stacked triple height with dirty dishes. He knew she had difficulty walking in a straight line at the best of times, to say nothing of carrying a fully laden tray. Yet, knowing this, he'd forgotten common sense. In his excitement to be done, he'd called out her name. This time, her accident was his fault for distracting her. It had been when she looked at him that she walked into the table.

Just thinking about it made his chest tighten and his heart pound. Out of the corner of his eye, he ignored propriety and peeked down at her leg. Sure enough, her skirt had crept up as she sat, showing a huge bruise in vivid shades of blues and greens.

As clearly as if it had just happened, he again visualized her expression, the horror, the embarrassment, and the pain of impact. In front of everyone present, she'd blinked the tears back, choked out an apology, and insisted on cleaning up the mess by herself. When he offered to help, she shook her head and turned her back to him while she collected the broken pieces onto the tray on the floor by herself.

He felt like he'd been sucker-punched in the gut.

It suddenly dawned on him that the sanctuary had grown silent. The pastor closed his eyes and raised his arms, then instructed everyone to bow their heads to pray.

Quickly, he put his arm around Chantelle, both to steady her as he woke her up, but mostly as a precaution to hold her down if she jumped from being startled.

He was about to give her a gentle shake, but he didn't want her to wake up quite yet.

Taking advantage of everyone having their eyes closed, he studied her, possibly, first because she wasn't looking back, and second, because it wasn't often that Chantelle was still. If she weren't walking, she was fidgeting or at least playing with her hair. Because of her small size and almost continual cycle of motion, he often compared her to an insect, always buzzing around but never settling down.

Another person who shared the same hyper trait of constant motion was Joe, only Joe was a more normal size.

Mark's stomach took a nosedive. Joe had been home from the hospital for only a few days, temporarily confined to bed or low levels of activity because of his heart attack.

For now, Chantelle was still young—but how many years of

the same hyperactive behavior and bad eating habits would it take for her to drive herself into the same situation? She'd already nearly fainted, and she said it hadn't been the first time.

The thought that something might happen to her stabbed him where he didn't think he could heal. For all her frenzied behavior, she did have a sweet heart and a helpful spirit. She often went out of her way to help others, sometimes to her own detriment. Unfortunately, her compassion for others tended to make her a poor supervisor. She tried her best, but she was completely unable to take a hard line, especially on questionable issues. Nor could she provide direction when she didn't know the answer herself. In only a week, he'd already seen her fold a couple of times when dealing with the employees.

On the other hand, for such a little shrimp, she somehow managed to hold her own against big, bad, rowdy customers. Not that a family restaurant like Joe's Diner attracted many of the unruly crowd; but on Saturday afternoon, a small group of young men came in who had obviously had a few drinks too many after a local sporting event. They had barely been seated when they became very loud and started to harass the part-time server. Mark had started to walk to their table to ask them to leave. However, before he could get there, Chantelle stomped up to their table and demanded that they apologize to the poor girl.

After listening to her rant and rave, they did apologize. But that wasn't enough for Chantelle. She didn't leave their table until they agreed that, after their dinners, Chantelle would call a cab, and they would come back later for their cars, when they were in better shape to drive. Still, she didn't quit. In the end, one of them ended up saying he would think about going to church on Sunday.

They even left a large tip.

She hadn't even thought about it. She jumped right in and hit the problem head-on, without planning or forethought, and won. When she needed to be strong, she was. But, for now, the warrior was a child, sleeping like a baby.

The pastor began to wind down his overlong prayer, so Mark thought it best that he wake Chantelle before everyone started moving. He planted his left hand firmly on her shoulder and shuffled slightly sideways. Very gently, he brushed Chantelle's cheek with the fingers of his right hand, taking his chances that she wouldn't do something to embarrass them both. "Chantelle," he whispered. "Wake up. Don't move."

Her eyes flickered open, and her head bobbed up so fast he wondered if she might have given herself whiplash. She inhaled sharply.

"Shhh. . . ," he whispered. "You fell asleep. The sermon is over. Everyone is praying."

Her eyes crossed slightly and her head swayed. The second her eyes focused on his face, she stiffened. "Mark? Oh, no," she whimpered. "I'm so embarrassed."

"Shhh. . ."

The congregation mumbled an "amen" in unison, and the pastor's voice rang out with the most volume and voice inflection Mark had heard in the past forty-seven minutes. "Everyone, please stand and we'll sing our closing song."

Mark let his arm drop as Chantelle stood.

The words to the song appeared on the screen, and the worship team began to play. Fortunately, he knew the song, so he sang along; but he didn't pay attention to the words as they came out of his mouth. Instead, he listened to Chantelle beside him. He hadn't noticed in the earlier part of the service, but except for a few notes that she missed, she had a lovely voice.

"Go in the peace of Christ!"

Numbly, he turned to Chantelle. She opened her mouth, but he didn't want to hear that she intended to drop him off at his parents' house and not see him again until Monday, back at the diner.

He rammed his hands in his pockets. "Can I take you out for lunch?"

Her eyes widened, and her mouth snapped shut. She reached down, picked up her purse, fumbled with it, and then popped a mint into her mouth. "I don't know. I can't think straight. I think I should just call it a day and go home. After I drop you off, of course."

"No!" Mark paused, cleared his throat, and lowered his voice. "I mean, I have an idea. Instead of going to a restaurant, why don't we go back to my parents' house, make a couple of sandwiches, and go sit in the park and enjoy the sunshine?"

Her brows knotted, and her whole face pinched as if she thought he were crazy for making such a suggestion. "Are you serious?"

He broke out into a full smile. He'd said the first thing that came into his head that didn't involve going to a restaurant. Now that the words were said, the appeal of sitting quietly in the park with Chantelle increased exponentially. "Yes. I think it would be great to just sit and take it easy for a couple of hours and not have to think about anything except grass stains."

"I don't know. . . ."

"Come on. I think we need the break."

Her eyes widened, and she stared up at him. He watched the interplay of thought flitter across her face, from surprise to disbelief, slowly changing into a charming, pretty smile. "You know, I think that's a great idea."

He smiled back. "Let's get going, then."

eleven

Halfway to Mark's parents' house, Chantelle finally realized what she was doing. She decided she really was too tired to function properly.

If Mark had not been driving her car, she wouldn't have believed what they were about to do or that she'd agreed to it.

As if she hadn't seen enough of the man in the past ten days, now she was going to spend the rest of her only free day with him, too. Worst of all, she couldn't remember the last time she'd been so embarrassed. She hadn't been aware of falling asleep, but she sure remembered waking up.

Once again, she had found herself wrapped in Mark's arms. Only this time, it wasn't a good-night "We did great today" hug in the privacy of the middle of the night, hidden behind her car. They were in church, in broad daylight, in a crowd of people. People she knew.

She wrestled with her feelings for Mark. In fleeting moments, when she allowed herself to dwell on her honest emotions, she longed to think of him as more than just a friend. Still, she knew the chances of a future relationship with him were next to nil. He would be leaving soon; and if she weren't careful, he'd be leaving her behind to nurse a broken heart.

At the diner, they were constantly doing battle. In fun, of course, although there had been a time or two when she'd been so angry with him she could barely look in his direction. She took great consolation knowing that sometimes she got on his nerves, too. He won most of the time, but whenever she saw that she was getting her way, she pushed the point just a little more, just so he would know that she was right.

Today, though, there was no competition, no differences of

opinion over the way something should be done. No employees phoning in sick, setting them both off in a tizzy, and no little "accidents" to clean up. It was their day off. Sunday. The Lord's day. They weren't supposed to be thinking of work. Yet, at the same time, she had put two and two together. They'd once discussed how he used to work through entire weekends, which included Sundays.

Suddenly, Chantelle felt her heart stop. Her whole body went cold at the realization of why Mark wanted to be alone with her.

Uncle Joe knew she needed the job desperately. From him, she could take a little charity and more than a little forgiveness for her latest accident of the day. But Mark saw things from a different perspective. While he knew how much she needed the job, Mark's primary concern was the financial well-being of the diner. And, going a step farther, he had to account for the extra expenses she incurred.

As the week wore on, the more tired she got, the clumsier she became. To her utter embarrassment, she seemed to drop things or trip even more than usual, often when Mark was watching.

Suddenly, she knew why Mark wanted to go to the park where they could be alone, away from the other people at the diner. Mark wanted to have "a talk" about everything she'd broken. Maybe he would suggest taking it out of her salary, although it wouldn't be a deterrent. It would only make her more self-conscious and make matters worse.

"What kind of sandwich would you like? Mom always keeps her kitchen well stocked, and I'm sure we can come up with just about any kind of sandwich combination you want."

The sound of Mark's voice made her realize that she'd been staring out the window since they'd left church, which was probably very rude.

"I don't know. Anything except seafood. I'm allergic."

When he stopped the car at a red light, he turned to look at her. "I figure if we know ahead of time what we want, we'll work more efficiently and be out of my mom's kitchen and headed toward the park in record time. I want a ham on rye, no mustard, with cheese and lettuce."

Chantelle stifled a chuckle. It shouldn't have surprised her that, even on his one day off, he was still as efficient as ever. Chantelle made a mental note to learn from his example.

"How 'bout if I make us a thermos of coffee, too? I haven't had enough sleep. I didn't get a chance to take a nap this morning."

Chantelle gritted her teeth. As if she weren't embarrassed enough, she didn't need reminded of her latest stupid escapade.

They raced through their lunch preparations and were almost at the park when Chantelle realized that it would only have taken them a minute out of their way to run into her apartment for a blanket to sit on. Now, it was too late. They had arrived.

Mark led her to a semisecluded spot under a large tree at the edge of the playing field.

"I thought this would be more private than in the picnic area. Is this okay with you?"

Chantelle forced herself to smile. At least he was considerate enough to talk to her away from people so no one would see her tears. "Yes, it's fine."

"Let's have a seat. I'm starving."

Chantelle kicked off her sandals, lowered herself to the grass, and tucked her legs underneath herself. Mark sat cross-legged facing her.

She knew she was in trouble because he was looking at her funny.

She tried to keep her hands from shaking as she pulled the sandwiches out of the bag. Mark poured their coffee. When they were ready to eat, Chantelle folded her hands in her lap and waited. As expected, he shuffled nervously and remained silent.

"I've noticed this before. Why don't you say grace before you eat? Don't you believe in God?"

He toyed with his sandwich wrapper, not looking at her. "Of course I do."

"Then why don't you pray? I'm sorry for being so blunt about it, but I noticed you avoided saying prayers with the staff, too. What's wrong?"

"Nothing's wrong," he mumbled as he lifted a corner of his sandwich and peeked inside. "I'm just not good at saying prayers out loud."

She doubted that was the whole story. Every time they'd prayed together, he never looked comfortable, aloud or silent.

"Want to talk about it?"

"Not really."

"Then I'll pray for both of us."

Mark bowed his head. Chantelle thanked God for the food before them, as well as for the smooth operation of the diner until Jack and Uncle Joe returned. She ended with thanking God for Uncle Joe's life and a prayer for his quick recovery.

They began to eat, but Chantelle couldn't let it go. "I say a prayer for Uncle Joe every day. I pray for you, too."

Mark nearly choked on his sandwich. She wanted to reach over and pat him on the back, but she'd been told that, even though it was a natural reaction, it was the wrong thing to do.

"If you must know, I no longer believe in prayer."

"How can you say that?"

"Over the past few years, I really haven't had time to go to church much, and I also got out of the habit of praying regularly. And you know what? It didn't make a difference."

Chantelle couldn't believe her ears. "But God wants to hear our prayers. He doesn't always answer them right away or necessarily in the way we want, but He does listen."

"I don't know how to respond to that. When I started to pray again, instead of getting better, things got worse. I've given up on prayer. God does what He wants to do anyway.

Let's just change the subject, okay? I need to lease a car for a few months, and I need you to suggest somewhere I can go. Nothing extravagant, just something so I won't have to depend on everyone around me for a ride all the time."

He'd changed the subject so quickly, Chantelle couldn't think properly. "I don't mind giving you a ride."

"I know you don't, and I'm very grateful for your willingness to let me borrow your car or pick me up. But starting tomorrow, I won't have to spend so much time in the office. That will free up someone else in the kitchen, and hopefully we can shuffle some of the part-timers and cut down on both our hours. I really do need my own transportation. I also have to get some stuff shipped here. I'll have to make a few phone calls tonight and see what I can arrange."

They ate the remainder of their sandwiches in silence. When they finished, they packed up the wrappers and tucked everything back into the bag. Even though they were free to talk, unless Chantelle prompted Mark, he didn't say anything. Regardless of what was being said at the time, his words about no longer believing in prayer echoed through her head, as well as his words that his life was getting worse instead of better.

Even though they didn't see eye-to-eye on many things, she didn't want him to be unhappy. As his friend, she wanted to know what had caused him to stop praying in the first place. From there, she could work her way forward to see what in his life he thought was so bad that he didn't want to pray anymore.

One thing she did know about him was that he tended not to talk a lot. She had no doubt he would consider her questions prying, but then again, she *was* prying. Still, there was so much about him she wanted to know.

So, she questioned him, and he answered. In the process, she found out a lot that Uncle Joe hadn't told her.

Mark had a well-paying job—if he still had his job when he

got home—although he apparently worked very hard and very long hours.

He lived in a fairly new apartment in a high-rise tower. He had no struggles with his landlord or neighbors. The rent was reasonable, and he never had to worry about not paying on time.

His family was fine, even though they were admittedly far away. Still, he was so busy with his job that he didn't have time to miss them, except for holidays. He seemed to solve that problem by working through most holidays.

He seemed to be in good health. He was slim, but not too skinny. He didn't get much exercise, but he did take the stairs instead of the elevator once a day at work, so he wasn't completely out of shape.

She even garnered the courage to ask if a woman had broken his heart. The answer was negative. His last "serious" relationship was with a woman at his office, but they broke up when he became her supervisor.

She asked every question she could think of but came up with no real hardship or heartbreak in his life to explain his attitude. When she finally ran out of questions, he flopped down flat on his back, linked his fingers behind his head, and stared up at the tree above them. Since she had nothing better to do and since she wasn't getting anywhere talking to him, Chantelle did the same, just making sure to position herself carefully so as to preserve her modesty since she was wearing a skirt.

Together they watched the squirrels scampering and jumping from branch to branch until Mark's cell phone rang.

Mark answered the call lying on his back. He mumbled a few affirmatives, rolled to his side to face Chantelle, and propped himself up on one elbow. "Ellen invited us for dinner. She says they want to thank us for jumping in and taking over, but I think Joe wants to ask us how things are going. Wanna go?"

Chantelle's heart sank. She hadn't done it on purpose, but by talking about everything except the diner all afternoon, she'd unintentionally distracted Mark from the reason he wanted to spend the afternoon together in the first place. Now that the diner found its way back into their conversation, it was time to hear the bad news.

She gulped and forced herself to smile. "Sure. It will be nice to have a home-made meal for a change, especially when I don't have to cook it."

He nodded and confirmed arrangements, then flipped the phone shut. "I know what you mean. I eat a lot of takeout. I love a good home-cooked meal."

He hopped to his feet, bent at the waist, and reached down to Chantelle. "Come on. I'll help you up."

All she could do was stare up at him as he smiled and flexed his hand. After spending hours lounging on the grass together, allowing him to help her up seemed to hint at something she couldn't figure out. But, since she was apparently the only one affected, she reached out toward him.

Mark linked his fingers through hers, covered her hand with his other hand, and pulled her to her feet.

When she was standing, he didn't let go, forcing her to stand closer to him than she wanted to be.

She tipped her head back and looked up into his eyes. Way up. Since she was barefoot and he still wore his shoes, the height difference was now a full twelve inches.

He ran his thumb over her wrist. With the other hand, he gave a small squeeze. "Thanks for doing this. I can't remember the last time I've completely wasted a day. It felt good. By the way, it's your turn to drive."

All Chantelle could do was nod. She waited, standing in one spot, for him to let go.

He didn't. He only smiled down at her.

After a couple of minutes of silence, he finally spoke. "Aren't you going to put your shoes back on?"

"Not if you won't let go of my hand."

"Oh." He gave a rather lame laugh. "Sorry." He released his grip barely enough for Chantelle to slide her hand out of his.

She started to bend down to stick a finger under the strap of her sandal so she could slip her foot in, but froze. She was not in the privacy of her home. She was in the middle of the park, where it mattered how she bent over when wearing a skirt.

Standing in one spot, she tucked her toes into her sandal; but when she stepped down, instead of her foot sliding in, she squished the back of her sandal with her heel.

She needed to sit down or lean against a wall.

Or a tree. Chantelle turned around. The nearby trees were certainly sturdy enough, but all were surrounded by sticks and growths of bushes and other twiggy clumps and lumpy pieces of mulch. She wasn't walking barefoot through that.

Anything solid would have done, except the only thing big and solid nearby was Mark.

Recently she'd heard him in Jack's office, muttering about desperate times calling for desperate measures.

She was desperate.

"Don't move," she mumbled. Chantelle raised her hand, splayed one palm on his shoulder, and leaned on him. He tensed as she supported herself against his weight, but otherwise, he was as sturdy as she thought he would be.

As quickly as she could, she raised her foot and swished a finger behind her heel to lift the strap to the right place. Once she was successful, she turned and repeated the process for the other foot. The moment both feet were back firmly on the ground, she began to straighten. Suddenly, Mark's hand covered hers.

He grinned, showing those adorable crow's-feet at the corners of his eyes to their full potential. "Glad to be of service."

Something in her stomach fluttered. Words failed her.

Instead of releasing her hand, he lowered both their hands and linked his fingers into hers. "Let's go."

They walked to the car hand in hand, in complete silence. Mark didn't say a word until they reached Uncle Joe and Aunt Ellen's home, and that was only a reminder for her to lock the car door.

Uncle Joe looked better than he had in the hospital, but he still didn't look great. His cheeks were drawn, and he looked very tired. A few times, she could see that when Uncle Joe moved the wrong way, it irritated his broken rib. Every time it happened, his pain echoed in Mark's face.

After dinner, Chantelle offered to help with the dishes, but Aunt Ellen wouldn't hear of it. She hustled everyone out of the kitchen and told all three of them to stay in the living room.

Of course, Uncle Joe sat in his favorite recliner. Chantelle sat in her usual spot at the end of the couch next to the fireplace. Instead of sitting at the other end of the couch, Mark sat down next to her. He immediately told Uncle Joe about his new system for keeping track of the stock through each order at the cash register. Mark beamed when Uncle Joe admitted that computers might be good for something, after all.

But then, Uncle Joe began to ask more direct questions about the day-to-day operations, where the troubles really were. Unlike the last time, Chantelle could no longer distract him with stories of the funny things that happened. This time, he was asking specific questions about specific things, and she didn't know what to say. She didn't want Uncle Joe to worry that things weren't going as well as they should have been, but she couldn't lie.

When Uncle Joe pointedly asked about what shift she had chosen, she knew she was caught. She had just opened her mouth, about to admit that both she and Mark had been working from opening until closing all week when Mark's hand covered hers.

Words failed her.

Mark gave her hand a little squeeze. "We still haven't figured out permanent shifts. Until now, things have been a little hectic, with only one car between us. But tomorrow, Chantelle's going to help me get a leased car. We might even go shopping. Right, Chantelle?" He lifted her hand to his face and nudged his lips across her knuckles. Her heart thumped wildly in her chest at his touch. She'd never known him to be so bold, but she found herself enjoying this unexpected interchange.

"Yes," she choked out, hoping she sounded at least half-normal.

Uncle Joe's eyes nearly popped out of his head. Chantelle wondered if the shock of what Mark had done might have been too much for him. Her own heart was racing in double time.

"You're looking a little tired, and we don't want to bore you with all the little things that go on at the diner. I think we should go. Don't you think so, Chantelle?"

Mark stood, not letting go of her hand, forcing her to either stand as well or cause a scene in front of Uncle Joe.

Chantelle stood. "Yes. Of course," she muttered, still bewildered as to what had come over Mark.

Uncle Joe called Aunt Ellen, and they both saw Mark and Chantelle to the door. Mark didn't release her hand until they were beside the car, and she had to let go to get her keys out of her purse.

Her hands shook as she handed Mark her keys. "I think you'd better drive."

She didn't realize her mistake until it was too late. Instead of simply accepting the keys, he encompassed both the keys and her hand within his. "They're both watching through the blinds. Kiss me."

"What? Why?"

Instead of answering, he bent his head and brushed a soft kiss to her lips at the same time as he pulled the keys out of her limp fingers.

He stepped back and opened the door for her. "I think maybe you should quit standing there and get in the car."

She got in the car only because she didn't want her aunt

and uncle to keep staring.

As soon as they were away from the house, Chantelle turned to Mark. "W–why did you do that?"

He grinned. "It stopped him from asking more questions than we were prepared to answer, didn't it?"

"Not that. I meant outside."

"Because with both of them watching, I knew I was safe. And now that I'm driving your car, I'm still safe."

Chantelle felt her mouth drop open as she stared at him.

"Chantelle, this will give him something else to think about besides worrying about the diner."

"Couldn't you think of something else?"

"Nope. And I didn't see you coming up with any bright ideas."

Not another word was spoken until they arrived at Mark's parents' house. She had expected him to say something about the path of destruction she'd carved at the diner on Saturday night or any of the other times she'd broken something during the week, but he didn't. Earlier Brittany had told her it was generally accepted in the restaurant business that every day someone would break something. Still, the bottom line was that Chantelle had the highest percentage of breakage of all the staff.

They both exited the car at the same time. Chantelle walked around to get into the driver's door, but Mark didn't walk to the house. He stood beside the car, waiting for her. Since they hadn't just had an exhausting day at the diner, she doubted that they would separate with what seemed to have become a routine of a daily hug. She cringed inwardly, waiting for him to say what she knew he had to.

She purposely stayed a few feet away. "Was there something you wanted to say to me?"

His brows knotted. "You don't really have to help me lease a car, but if you want to go shopping with me, that might be fun, although I don't know about leaving the diner short staffed."

"Not that. All day long I've had the feeling that you wanted to say something to me."

He raised one eyebrow. "You did?"

"Yes. Yet, after we finished lunch, all we did was lie in the grass for an hour and look up at the sky. What were you thinking about?"

He grinned. "I was thinking of a way that I could kiss you. Maybe God does answer prayers."

Before Chantelle could think of an appropriate response, Mark turned and disappeared inside the house.

❧

"Thanks, and come again," Chantelle said as yet another family of satisfied customers left Joe's Diner.

As soon as the door closed behind them, Chantelle allowed herself the yawn she'd been fighting.

This week, as promised, Mark had spent more time in the kitchen than the office. He'd said the new system would shorten their hours, and it had. Instead of working from opening until closing, she had put in "only" twelve hours every day. Except, because everything wasn't so new and exciting, what was now becoming routine was wearing her down faster.

She couldn't remember ever being so tired in her life. The only good thing was that she didn't have to wait until closing. She could now go home after the supper rush was over, leaving Mark to watch things during the evenings, do the cleanup, and lock up, since he now had his leased car.

The only cheerful note was that tomorrow was Sunday. Even though she still had to get up for church, since she didn't have to get up with the birds to open the diner, she considered it sleeping in.

When the number of patrons dropped to the agreed number, Chantelle walked to the back to tell Mark she was leaving.

Instead of the kitchen, she found him in the office, working hard at the computer.

Chantelle stood in the doorway, leaned her shoulder into

the doorframe, crossed one ankle over the other, and crossed her arms. "I thought this week we were going to be able to work eight-hour shifts, but that hasn't happened. Uncle Joe said no overtime."

He nodded as he clicked the mouse and waited for his transaction to complete. "Technically, we're not doing overtime. I put us both on salary rather than hourly, so no matter how many hours we work, we'll get the same wage. In other words, we never get overtime, at least not paid overtime. Ideally, that's also supposed to work the same if we put in less than eight hours a day or even take a day off, but I think we both know that's not going to happen."

"No kidding. We really need another person."

Mark nodded as he entered more data. "I know. But reality dictates that since we have to pay ourselves, Joe's Diner can't afford it. The bottom line is to turn a profit, and it's on the edge now. That's another reason I put us on salary, to make our incomes fixed. I don't know how they did it, but I suspect Uncle Jack and Joe have been putting in an awful lot of extra hours over the years. They're also making a significant amount more than we are. But they're investors, too."

"I would never have thought this is what it takes to own and operate a business. I've always thought that people who owned their own business took lots of time off and went on exotic vacations."

Mark exited his program and pushed the mouse into the center of the mouse pad. "I know a boss who does just that. Sean. He made me do all his work; like a sap, I fell for it, suckered in by promises of future promotion and partnerships. I've worked hard with long hours like this for years. Only now, it's personal. It's easier to take because this time it's my own decision."

"I know what you mean. This is hard, but I don't mind doing it because it's for Uncle Joe. So, now that you've got your own car, and your clothes and stuff arrived yesterday, do you want me to pick you up for church tomorrow, or do you want to meet me there?"

"There's really no point in me going to church. What's going to change?"

"Change? I don't understand."

"I've been going to church faithfully all my life. I know I'm not destitute and out on the streets, but really, where am I in life? For the last few years it seems like all I've done is work, and I'm no further ahead than when I started, no matter what I do or how hard I try. On the way here, I prayed for a break, and now I'm working harder and longer than ever."

Chantelle couldn't hold back her gasp. "God doesn't promise us riches or success. He promises something better. Something lasting. Because you're a believer, He's given you the gift of salvation, which lasts for all eternity. Aren't you thankful for that?"

Mark mumbled something under his breath, but she didn't ask him to repeat himself. She walked into the office to stand beside him, behind the desk.

"Last weekend you mentioned something else you've been talking to God about."

His brows knotted, and he crossed his arms over his chest. "I did?"

Chantelle stepped closer, bent over, and rested her fingertips on his shoulder. "You said God answered your prayer because you wanted to kiss me." Before she thought about the ramifications of what she was doing, Chantelle brushed a quick kiss to Mark's cheek, then dashed around the desk and back to the safety of the office doorway. "Now not only did you get to kiss me last weekend, I just kissed you back. God really does answer prayers."

She spun around and looked at him over her shoulder, barely able to keep from laughing at his stupefied expression. "This time you can pick me up. I'll see you same time as last Sunday. Have a great evening. I'm going home."

twelve

Chantelle wasn't at the front when Mark arrived at the diner, allowing him to slip into the office without having to talk to her.

Once Chantelle got her mind stuck on something, not only was she like a dog with an old bone, she had taken persistence to new levels. First, he couldn't believe what she did in order to get him to church. Then, once they were there, she not only stayed awake through the pastor's boring sermon, but every few minutes she passed him a note commenting on the pastor's message. Periodically, she questioned him to clarify what the pastor had said.

Mark wasn't stupid. He knew she heard and understood everything perfectly. She was only making sure he was paying attention. The way she went about it grated on his nerves, but he refused to act like a child and not pay attention simply to get back at her. Her actions forced him to pay attention, in spite of himself. What annoyed him most of all was that her badgering worked. She knew it, too. He saw it in her self-satisfied attitude when they went to the park for lunch.

At lunch, he had to admit that he was proud of her. Not only had she packed a small cooler with sandwiches for their lunch, she had brought a blanket in anticipation of sitting on the grass again. She may not have been the most organized person in the world, but she was improving. That took away some of his annoyance at being dragged to church when he would rather have stayed in bed.

The computer just finished booting up when Chantelle appeared in the doorway.

"We have a problem. You know how I was saying that

we really need another person on staff? It appears we do. Apparently, Uncle Joe gave Esther some time off to move. She phoned about an hour ago, asking about her hours for the week. I didn't know what to say, so I told her to come in her regular time. She said she always starts at four-thirty, for the supper rush, until closing."

Mark ran his fingers through his hair. "How many days a week does she usually work?"

"She's full-time, Tuesday through Saturday, late shift."

He stared at his computer screen without really seeing it. The diner was at the limit of what they could afford in salaries. He could have Esther on staff for a few weeks, but any more than that, all it would take would be a few bad days, and over the course of a month, the diner would be paying out more money than it was taking in. "We really can't afford another person."

"I had a rather long talk with her after I told her what happened to Uncle Joe. She told me a little about herself. Mark, she's a single mother. She really needs the money. And she really does have a position here."

He buried his face in his hands. If Esther really were a regular employee, then the burden wasn't Esther, but himself and Chantelle. "Then we've got to find a way to increase business to offset the additional expense."

"You mean some kind of special promo to get more people coming in?"

"Yes, but effective advertising costs a lot of money, which makes it even harder."

"You mean we've got to spend money to make money?"

He nodded. "Exactly."

They stared at each other in silence, Mark's mind running a mile a minute. Except for recently, he'd only spent time in the kitchen. He knew nothing about running a restaurant. He knew less about how to promote one. "How come you didn't know about this extra person and that she was coming back to work this week?"

Chantelle crossed her arms and scrunched her eyebrows. "When she called, I knew I'd heard the name before, but it didn't click until she said she was all settled in her new house. Uncle Joe mentioned that he gave her some time off when he phoned me the day of Jack's accident. That also explains why we've been feeling so shorthanded. We are shorthanded."

"Great. What a way to find out."

"I have to get back to the front. We're starting the lunch rush, and I've left Brittany alone. I'll come back if I think of something."

She walked away without further comment, leaving Mark one more problem to worry about. He called up the database to study their peak periods, hoping to get some ideas before he had to run off and start his scheduled time in the kitchen.

Just as he finally found the file that showed breakdowns of inventory on a monthly basis for the previous year, Chantelle appeared in the doorway.

"Could we still make money if we offered ten percent off all our meals? I mean for a limited time period."

Mark shrunk the program, called up another one, and punched in a few figures.

"If we made up for it in volume, yes, I suppose we could."

"Great. Thanks."

She turned and disappeared without elaborating.

Mark shrugged his shoulders, cleared the data, and called up the past year's monthly inventory stats again. He then called up the current month's inventory and tried to make a comparison, estimating the last week in the month that made the current month's data incomplete.

Chantelle appeared in the doorway again. "What if we had a weekly drawing or something for a free dinner for one family up to four or five people? Could we afford to do that?"

Mark shrank the two files he had open, recalled the one he had previously opened, and punched in a few numbers.

"Yes. Again, if the volume increased to warrant the cost."

She disappeared again, this time without commenting.

He killed the file, called up what he had been looking at previously, and tried to remember how far he'd gotten in his estimate for the current month.

Chantelle appeared in the doorway again.

"Could we afford to run an ad or two in the local newspaper that comes out twice a week?"

"I don't know. It depends what it costs."

She glanced over her shoulder at the sound of another group of people coming in through the main door. "I'm kind of busy. Can you phone and find out?"

Mark opened his mouth, but she disappeared before he could say anything.

"And I'm not busy?" he asked the empty doorway.

When the doorway didn't reply, Mark sighed, pulled out the phone book, and made the inquiries.

When Chantelle appeared again, he had her answers, both as to cost and a cautious estimate that, based on a certain percentage of increased sales, they could run one ad in the weekend paper, then again in the midweek paper.

"Okay," she said and disappeared again.

This time, Mark shrank only the program he used for allocating cost per servings. She'd be back. He knew it.

He just discovered that they were possibly heading into a seasonal slump when the blond bombshell materialized in the doorway again.

"How about if we ran an ad for a contest that we could have going for the next month and gave away four free meals, one per week, for a prize? That way we could get the benefit of the paid advertising for the first week and hope for the word-of-mouth advertising for the next three weeks."

"It would have to be a pretty good contest to be able to recoup our costs. Those ads are expensive."

One corner of her mouth quirked down, the tip of her tongue appeared in the other corner, which turned up, and one eye closed. "Hmm. . . ," she said and disappeared again.

Mark shook his head. The woman was making him dizzy.

When she didn't come back, he saved his work to a temporary file and hurried to the kitchen.

He was in the middle of making an omelet when Chantelle appeared, leaning over the counter where they placed the orders to be delivered. "Do you own a digital camera?"

He didn't look up. "Yes, I do."

"I hope you had it packed and shipped with your stuff."

This time he did look up. "Yes, I did."

"What about software? Could I transfer pictures from it onto my computer?"

He transferred the omelet to a plate, added a scoop of hash browns, and slid the plate onto the counter directly in her direction, forcing her to move. "No, of course I didn't have Josh pack the software. But I have the software loaded onto my laptop, and I have the cable hookup in my laptop case."

"Do you think your laptop is compatible with my printer?"

"Probably."

Her eyes lit up, and she smiled so brightly, he imagined the room got lighter. "Great!" she singsonged, clapped her hands together, and skipped off, returning to the front of the restaurant.

Kevin froze beside him. The two men turned and looked at each other. "Uh-oh. . . ," they mumbled in unison.

❧

Mark shook his head and backed up a step. "No. I'm not wearing that. No way. Never. Not in a million years."

Chantelle held out the most ghastly excuse for a hat he'd ever seen in his life. The thing looked like a cross between a fishing derby and an ecological waste dump.

"I don't need you to wear it long. Just a minute or two."

"Well. . ." He let his voice trail off as he considered her request. He wouldn't be caught dead wearing such a monstrosity in public; but if she only wanted him to try it on, he supposed he could do that.

"Just long enough for Aunt Ellen to take our picture."

His stomach took a nosedive into his shoes. "No. Absolutely not."

"But you have to. It's for the ad. Everyone who isn't working right now is coming in on their days off just for this picture. Please?"

"Pardon me?"

"This is for our contest. On Monday, we're starting Crazy Hat Month. For everyone who wears a crazy hat, they get ten percent off their meal. I ordered a big bulletin board, and we'll post a picture of everyone who wears a crazy hat, with their permission of course. Then on the weekend, everyone who comes in, whether they buy a meal or not, gets to vote on the craziest hat of the week. The winner will get a free meal for their family."

"You're crazier than that ugly hat."

"And if we bought a package of that expensive photo paper, I wonder if we might be able to sell the pictures to people. Or better yet, we can put a jar on the front counter. If anyone wants to buy a picture, they can put a dollar into the jar for charity. Like the children's hospital burn unit or something."

"You are crazy. Very crazy. And I thought we were going to discuss what we were going to do for promo."

Her smile dropped. "But we did discuss it. You said okay to the ten percent off, and to running a contest, and to running two ads." She held up the camera. "You gave me your camera. You even told me we could use your laptop to process the pictures right away."

"But—"

Ellen stepped forward and removed the camera from Chantelle's hand. "Come on, Mark. It will be fun."

He looked at Ellen, and all resistance drained out of him. Joe still wasn't up to coming to the diner, but Ellen had come, apparently just to take the picture.

Chantelle stepped forward and laid her hand on Mark's

forearm. "Everyone's waiting for us outside. Those who are working today have to get back to work, and everyone else is here on their day off. Please? We have to make this fast."

"I give up," he muttered and accepted the hideous hat. Still, even though he had agreed, he refused to wear the hat except for the amount of time it took for Ellen to snap the photograph.

His breath caught when he saw all the staff outside, all wearing their uniforms, along with a profound variety of very crazy hats.

Chantelle tugged on his sleeve. "Come on. I've got the ad all made up, but you've got to download the picture and format it properly for me really fast. Deadline is at three-thirty this afternoon for Sunday's paper. I thought it would be a great shot to have everyone standing in the doorway so we can get the Joe's Diner sign in the picture, too.

Mark forced himself to smile as everyone positioned themselves, not by height, but by where they could stand without their hats clashing with that of the person next to them.

"Aren't these hats great?" Chantelle whispered in his ear when they were done.

Mark whipped the hat off his head, then winced when he pinched his palm with a fishing hook. "I'm beginning to seriously question your taste. What makes you think this bizarre idea will work?"

"Just think. This is a family restaurant. Parents can keep the kids out of their hair for a few hours by having them make their hats. On the weekends, lots of teens come in because we're affordable, and wearing a crazy hat gives them an excuse to do something wild and crazy without getting out of hand. And while I'm thinking of it, do you think we can allow people to enter more than once in a week, as long as they have a different hat?"

Mark shrugged his shoulders, past the point of caring anymore. "Why not? The purpose of this thing is to draw a crowd. If someone is crazy enough to make more than one hat in a week, they deserve to get a discount off their meal."

"One more thing. You don't have to, but everyone else is going to wear their hat during working hours to keep in the mood of the contest."

"Everyone?"

"Yes. Everyone."

Mark stared at Chantelle, wearing a wide-rimmed beach hat that she'd made into a real beach. She'd made the rim into the water, complete with blue waves, jumping fish, swimming birds, and a doll on a surfboard. The crown was a sandy island sticking out of the water, complete with a palm tree and a sun sticking up on a wire protruding from the top of the palm tree. Beside the palm tree was a badly constructed hotdog stand, made from cardboard and a picture she'd cut out of a magazine.

"You made that, didn't you?"

She beamed, like it was something to be proud of. "Yes!"

He stared blankly at the monstrosity in his hand, telling himself that nothing was worse than Chantelle's hat. Being in the kitchen, hardly anyone would see him. He hadn't lived here for four years, so he doubted anyone he knew would see him. If they did, they would have seen Chantelle first, and nothing was as bad as that. At least the hat she'd made for him was at one time a proper fishing hat. Something macho and respectable.

"You win. But do me a favor. Don't skip. Walk nice and calm, and let's get back to work."

&a.

While he waited for Chantelle to pick him up for church, Mark picked up the local community newspaper from the front step. The sight of the front page nearly made his heart stop.

Local Restaurant Goes Crazy

In full, vivid color, on the front page, was a photo of a large group of people, all wearing ridiculous hats, standing by the front door of Joe's Diner. The first few lines of the article clarified the title with the name of the contest. He studied the sea of faces carefully. Not one of the people in the picture was a staff member. He wondered if any of the staff knew about the picture, because no one had told him another picture had been taken.

Quickly, he paged through to page five to read the rest of the feature article.

Today marked the end of the second week of the contest. Inside was a picture of the fifty-ish man who won the prize for the first week, holding up the gift certificate they had presented to him. He was grinning from ear to ear and wearing a hat sporting a racetrack around the brim, complete with cars that drove in a big circle around the hat when the man moved his head.

Mark didn't want to think of how many hours the man and others like him had spent making ridiculous hats for the sake of a lousy ten-percent discount off the price of an already reasonable meal. When Chantelle handed the man his prize, he said that he hadn't really expected to win and that the prize was a bonus he hadn't even considered. He'd simply had fun making the hat and even more fun wearing it.

The article also mentioned the charity jar. About half the people who had worn hats wanted to keep a picture of themselves, and they'd been more than happy to donate a dollar to a worthy cause in exchange for a copy of the picture.

A car horn honked. Mark jumped and looked up to see Chantelle in her car, waiting at the curb.

"Sorry, I didn't see you pull up. I was reading the morning paper." He handed her the newspaper before she slipped the car into gear. "Did you have anything to do with this? I notice they quoted you. Why didn't you tell me?"

Chantelle's mouth gaped open when she looked at the picture on the front page. "I didn't know. The newspaper phoned and asked me a few questions, but no one told me they were going to use it for an article. I just thought their advertising department was phoning as a follow-up to see if we wanted to run another ad. Which I didn't." She laid the paper into her lap and grinned at him. "You've got to admit, we've been busy. After hitting the front page, we're bound to be busy until the contest is over. There's no such thing as bad publicity."

"I guess not."

"Well, what do I get? You told me you didn't think this would work, but I proved you wrong. I win! I think you should give me something."

Mark gazed into her face. Since they no longer drove to work together, by the time he arrived, she was already wearing one of the ridiculous hats that she'd made to promote the contest. None of them did her justice. All they did was make her look silly, which he supposed was the point. She hadn't cared that the hats were unflattering. She wanted only to bring people into the diner, and her plan had worked. For the past two weeks, they'd had record crowds and often had a wait in nonpeak hours.

Today, just as she had on every other Sunday, Chantelle wore a minimum of makeup. Instead of a bizarre hat, she wore a large, stylish clip to hold her hair in place in such a way that accentuated her diamond-shaped face and rosy cheeks. Her blue eyes sparkled with delight, and her beautiful smile could have competed with a fully lit Christmas tree if it hadn't been the wrong time of year. Crooked nose aside, she radiated pure joy and an inner beauty beyond description.

What he wanted to give her was a kiss. But he couldn't.

"Mark? Is something wrong? Why are you looking at me like that? Do I have something stuck on my face?"

Mark blinked a couple of times and shook his head. "No. Sorry. Let's go. We shouldn't be late."

"I forgot to tell you. Uncle Joe is going to church today. He invited us to go with him, to his church, and then go over to their place for lunch afterward."

"Sure. Why not?"

This time, Mark found himself paying attention to the sermon without Chantelle's prompting or her infamous question-and-answer periods. The reason wasn't only that he found the pastor at their uncles' church much more interesting than the pastor at Chantelle's church.

The pastor's topic was the eternal life promised to those who accepted Jesus as their personal Lord and Savior. Of course, he'd known that since he was a child. He'd been brought up in church. But today, Chantelle's words about God not promising anything else besides salvation echoed in his head. At first, he simply listened politely as the pastor spoke, but when the pastor read a verse where Jesus Himself promised that future Christians would have troubles throughout their lives, that was when Mark really started paying attention.

He'd been thinking a lot about his life in the last couple of weeks. It had started when Chantelle flooded him with questions when they were at the park. At the time, he'd simply answered, thinking that she had the strangest way he'd ever seen of getting to know someone. When Mark got to know someone, he learned by observation, not with a barrage of personal questions, one right after the other.

But in answering her questions, he had to think about his replies.

For everything she'd asked, regardless of the personal nature of the question, something in his reply had to do with his job. Most people in today's society spent more time at their job than anything else in their life besides sleeping, including family time. However, in talking about it, he saw that his entire life revolved around his job, including his social life and what little was left of his spiritual life. Of course, he still believed the Bible and everything God said. But for the past number of years, Mark hadn't lived the way he believed.

Somewhere along the line, he'd stopped living for the God of the universe and started using all his time and energy to serve the god of his job. In doing so, he'd cut himself off from everything else in his life that should have been important. Everything revolved around his work. Without that job, he'd lost his anchor. And that made him realize that he was holding the wrong anchor. The problem wasn't that God wasn't answering his prayers. His problem was that he was serving the wrong god.

Not that he expected God to solve all his troubles once he turned himself around. The pastor's message confirmed that, which he already knew. Christians still had to face problems, maybe more than the average nonbeliever. Things would still continue to go wrong. But now, for the first time, it finally sank in that even when things did go wrong, he could still have peace because at the end of it all, no matter what happened, God promised him the gift of eternal life. Nothing else mattered.

At the close of the service, instead of following the pastor's prayer, which was more geared toward the new believer, Mark did something he hadn't done in a long time. Instead of asking God to fix his problems and listing the things he'd like changed, Mark opened his heart and told God that he would try his best to be open. From now on, Mark promised he would spend less time working and more time listening to whatever it was that God was trying to tell him. And then, he would do it.

"Amen!" the pastor called out. "Go! In the peace of Christ!"

Because it was Joe's first time back to church since his heart attack, Ellen, Mark, and Chantelle tried their best to get him home quickly, before he could get too tired. He protested, saying that he could handle church just fine if he was already starting a light exercise regime. However, his arguments fell on deaf ears as they escorted him all the way to his car. Joe even grumbled that he was quite ready to start driving again, but Ellen hushed him with a simple narrowing of her eyes while she started the car.

Mark then followed Chantelle to her car and, unlike Joe, slid into the passenger side without complaint.

Instead of staring out the window the entire drive to Joe and

Ellen's home, Mark watched Chantelle.

He'd been watching her closely, studying her, and most of all, getting to know her. There was more to Chantelle than the bubbly, animated little blond that everyone came to know and love. And everybody did love her. Since she worked such long hours at the diner and didn't have time to see her friends, her friends had come to see her. In fact, they accounted for a noticeable portion of the diner's business, with or without silly hats.

Watching her interact with her friends showed a side of Chantelle that he, at first, had been too self-absorbed to see.

He'd already known that she'd only held data-entry and low-level office jobs prior to working at Joe's Diner and that she'd been out of work for six months before Joe hired her at the diner. What he hadn't thought of was what being out of work with minimal education and training had really meant in day-to-day life.

She hadn't realized that there was a one-week holdback on payday at the diner, which put payday on the fourth day of the month. If she would have asked him for an advance, he gladly would have given it to her or even given her a personal loan, but she hadn't said a word. He didn't realize just how broke she was until a group of her friends came in and left an extremely large tip, saying that since it was a tip, she couldn't turn it down. She'd broken down and cried, saying that she now could pay the rest of her rent, which was overdue.

Mark couldn't imagine not having enough money to pay the rent. He also couldn't imagine not having enough money to pay for groceries; yet one day, when she'd invited him inside her home for coffee, he discovered the hard way that the cupboards were nearly bare. Apparently, one reason Chantelle didn't mind working long hours six days a week at the diner was because her meals were paid for and all she had to have on hand was what she needed for breakfast and nothing else.

Mark's cupboards at his apartment were often bare because

he didn't have the time to go grocery shopping, never because he didn't have the money to spend.

Using Chantelle's own bizarre methods of getting to know someone, Mark asked her a few carefully worded questions. He found out that, after being out of work for six months, she not only had spent all her savings, she'd cashed in her small retirement savings plan, and her debts were mounting to the point where she could no longer obtain any more credit.

As soon as he learned this, Mark had immediately tried to give her money, but she'd refused him. Again, he used Chantelle's own methods and worked around her.

Once a week he made an excuse to borrow her car, then filled up her gas tank while he was out. Mark smiled to himself as he recalled her confusion when she commented that she was surely losing her mind, that she couldn't remember the last time she had to buy gas. He'd also taken it through the quickie-lube place for a complete tune-up during one of his trips to the wholesaler. The following day she'd mentioned how the car "felt" different, but he wouldn't admit what he'd done. He admitted only to filling up the tank with premium gas and quickly changed the subject. Another time, he'd gotten all the brake pads changed and rotated the tires. He wanted to give her more, but for now it was a start.

He also learned that, unlike his, her family life wasn't stable. His parents had been happily married for thirty-five years, while her parents were divorced. The only other time he'd seen Chantelle cry was when she told him that her father had never been a Christian. Instead of hanging onto the Lord for strength after the divorce, her mother fell away completely. Nothing Chantelle could say or do had been able to bring her mother back into God's fold.

He couldn't believe that he'd been so direct, but following Chantelle's own methods, he also bluntly asked if she had anyone to call special and why not. Again, her answer surprised him.

When she was in her early twenties, she'd been engaged. She had caught her fiancé, who was supposed to be a devout Christian young man, cheating on her, and that ended the relationship. Chantelle, being Chantelle, didn't let herself become bitter over the experience. She told him that she often dated and that one day she hoped to find her Mr. Right. As of yet, God hadn't shown her the man with whom she would cross paths.

When that happens—somewhere, someday—someone will be a very lucky man.

"Here we are!" Chantelle chirped as she pulled into Joe's driveway. "You've been so quiet all the way here. What were you thinking?" Instead of leaving the car, she sat in the seat, not so patiently waiting for him to tell her everything, which he had no intention of doing.

Mark smiled. "Just stuff. We'd better go inside. Ellen and Joe will think it rather strange if we just sit in the driveway."

"Probably. And this time, don't tell me to lock the door. This isn't the big city. It's little Aidleyville. My car is quite safe in the driveway, even with the windows down."

He smiled again. Her boundless optimism and zeal for life in general were wearing off on him. He wasn't going to tell her that his own car had been broken into and vandalized in the supposedly-secure underground parking at his apartment complex not long before he left. Because Chantelle said so, here in little Aidleyville, her car and its contents probably were quite safe.

"You win. Let's go in."

thirteen

Chantelle tried not to let her mouth hang open as she stared at Mark. "What have you done to your hair?"

"That's a long story. I went in for a simple haircut, but the stylist convinced me that this would look really good. I've never done anything wild before, so I thought I'd give it a try."

Chantelle leaned over the counter toward him for a closer look. "I don't believe this. You got your hair streaked."

"The stylist called it a foil. Anyway, even though summer is over, I think it gives me that 'I've just been on vacation' look. Since I didn't get my vacation, getting my hair to look like I just got back from a month in the tropics is the next best thing. Do you like it?"

All Chantelle could do was nod. The blond highlights were quite vivid against his natural brown. It shouldn't have suited him, but it did.

Over the past few months, she'd seen many changes in him, but this one topped them all. Of course, hearing that he'd been to the Wednesday night service was better than anything he could have done to his hair.

She'd been extremely happy when he started being the first to mention going to Sunday services, and now, to hear that he'd not only gone to the Wednesday night service without her suggesting it, but that he'd gone alone, she didn't know what to think.

Immediately after Uncle Joe's first time back to church, Mark had changed their working hours. First, he cut them both down to a five-day workweek instead of six. Neither of them got two days off in a row, but in addition to having Sunday off for the Lord's day, she now got Tuesday off, and

Mark took Wednesday off. In addition to the shorter work-week, since business remained good after their hat contest ended, Mark hired another part-time server, which allowed them both to work only eight hours a day, Chantelle taking the early shift of opening to two-thirty, and Mark taking the second shift of one-thirty to closing.

At first, she liked the idea, because shortening her time at the diner gave her the rest of her life back. However, she hadn't expected to feel regret at not seeing Mark so much. With an overlap of only an hour in the middle of the day, they hardly saw each other anymore during the week. She found herself coming into the restaurant on Tuesday, making up excuses just so she could talk to him. Of course, when he came on Wednesdays, his day off, to talk to her, he had legitimate reasons for being there. The time she saw the most of Mark was Sunday, when they spent the afternoon alone together after church and most of the time Sunday evenings as well.

"By the way," he said now, bringing her back to the present. "You were right. That service at Joe's church on Wednesday night was really something."

"That's great," she said, so confused that she couldn't think of anything else to say.

"Why don't you come with me next Wednesday? You're off halfway through the day. I'll take you home right after it's over so you can get enough sleep to be up early Thursday. I think you'd really like it. I also saw that friend of yours, Jennifer. We sat together. She liked my hair."

Jennifer was there. He'd been with Jennifer. Something in Chantelle's stomach knotted, making her realize that she was hungrier than she thought. "Sure. We can do that."

Mark stepped closer. He plunked his elbows on the counter beside the cash register and leaned forward. "You know, I was thinking."

Chantelle cringed. When Mark thought something, whatever

it was, good or bad, it always came to pass.

"Things have been going really well, but we really should take more time to go over the loose ends. We hardly see each other anymore. We should schedule a time to sit down and talk. We haven't done any promotions besides your Crazy Hat Month. That worked so well, we should think of something else. Only this time, I'd like to participate a little in the planning."

Chantelle grinned sheepishly. "I guess," she mumbled.

"The only time we're here at the same time is from one-thirty to two-thirty, so let's put that hour aside for just the two of us to sit in the office and talk. Over lunch."

A small group of people walked in, giving Chantelle only enough time to nod her agreement. Mark straightened, winked, and walked away, whistling.

Whistling. He'd winked at her.

Chantelle pinched herself just to make sure she wasn't dreaming.

As soon as she seated the recent arrivals, she signaled to Brittany to take over hosting and ran into the office, where she found Mark busily working on the new computer.

She stood in the doorway, not sure if she should interrupt him. "I haven't had lunch yet. Have you? Would you like to start those meetings today?"

He hit save and leaned back in the chair. "That sounds like a good idea." He pushed the button for the intercom to the kitchen. "Kevin, can you please make up a couple of lunches for me and Chantelle? We'll both have the weekly special. Thanks."

Knowing that Kevin would buzz them back when their lunches were ready, Chantelle lowered herself into the padded chair beside the desk. "Do you know it's been nearly four months since Uncle Joe's heart attack?"

Mark lifted his arms and linked his fingers behind his head. "I know. We got off to a bit of a rocky start, but I think we've done quite well. Profits are up, and that's after taking into account the additional salaries."

Chantelle looked around the office. It was still Jack's office; but over the last four months, Mark had added his own personal touches. The most noticeable change was that everything looked spotlessly clean and meticulously organized.

The only thing slightly out of place was a large yellow Post-it note stuck to the side of the monitor with a Bible verse on it.

> *"I have told you these things, so that in me you may have peace. In this world you will have trouble. But take heart! I have overcome the world."*
>
> —John 16:33

"I wonder what's going to happen when Jack and Uncle Joe come back. Do you think they'll be able to use that new program you installed for doing the stock and ordering?"

"Probably. It's very user-friendly."

"I don't know if I'm still going to have a job here. Uncle Joe will do the hosting. That means the only way I'll be able to stay is if Uncle Joe were to let go the two part-time people we hired and I went back to serving, which I'm not very good at."

"That's still almost a month away. Don't worry about it. All you can do is pray about it and wait for an answer. Maybe you'll get that job at the bank that you wanted."

Something did a flip-flop in Chantelle's chest. To know that Mark was again praying did her heart a world of good, but to have him suggest to her that she pray for something and wait for God's direction seemed like a miracle. She still didn't know what happened to open his heart again to God's leading; but whatever it was, she praised God for it.

Mark leaned sideways, lifted the page on the calendar, and tapped his finger to the new page. "We really should go over the menus. Now is the time to plan for whatever's going to happen for the Thanksgiving season, whether we're here or not, because we need to start placing orders. There's decorating to do, too. Do you think we should go with a turkey decor or dried vegetables?"

"They usually go with the vegetables, but maybe if we do turkeys, we can plan a contest and—"

Brittany's voice blared over the intercom. "Call for you on line two, Mark."

Mark sighed. "That's probably the supplier. I ordered chicken burgers, and they sent me turkey. Excuse me." He hit the button to put the call over the speaker and began punching in keys to open the program for the stock. "Mark Daniels," he said in the direction of the phone on the desk. "How can I help you?"

The voice that came over the phone wasn't Stan.

"Mark? It's Mom. A letter came for you today, and I thought I should call rather than wait for you to come home tonight. It's from S&B."

Mark made a typo on his password, and his hands froze. He gulped and looked up at Chantelle. "Open it."

The sound of a staticky rip crackled over the speaker. Both of them heard his mother gasp. "It's a check. And it's a big one. Oh, Mark. . ." Her voice trailed off.

Chantelle forced herself to breathe. *A severance check.* After all this time, now they knew. When Jack and Uncle Joe came back, both of them would be looking for a new job.

"And there's a letter. . . . 'Dear Mark,' " his mother read flatly. " 'Enclosed is a check for all unused vacation time, the payout for accumulated unused sick time, plus pay at time-and-a-half rate for weekends worked, as submitted. Subsequent to our conversation in which you advised me of your notice of a leave of absence and contrary to your suggestion, I took your request to the board. This matter has been under consideration since then, pending a committee decision. During that time, it was discovered that we had neglected to give you a promised increase in salary. Therefore, also included in this amount is the difference in salary, retroactive to the date of agreement. This check now pays out all monies owed to you as of the current date.' "

His mother paused.

Mark grinned weakly. "How about that? I got a raise."

Chantelle tried to smile and couldn't. "Yeah."

His mother continued. "Please be advised that your position, at the new rate of pay, can be made available to you, pending your reply within thirty days from the date of this letter. Upon acceptance, we offer a one-month signing bonus as further incentive. We look forward to hearing from you. Regards, Sean McCafferty.' Mark! You've still got your job!"

Mark's face paled. "Excuse me," he muttered to Chantelle as he picked up the receiver and clicked it off the speaker setting. "How much is the check, Mom?"

His face paled even more. "Yeah. Great. Thanks. See you later. Bye."

Chantelle waited in silence until Mark was able to speak.

His voice came out in a hoarse croak. "They must really want me back. I didn't expect this."

Chantelle stood. For a reason she couldn't explain, she'd mentally logged the date of Mark's phone call to his boss. She thought it no coincidence that the thirty-day deadline for the letter was exactly five months from that date. "Maybe I should leave you to think about it."

Mark jumped to his feet. "Please. Don't go. I can't rush this. They're dangling quite a carrot in front of me, but I don't know that I can go back to working on their terms. I've been down that road before, and I have to think about my options. Most of all, I have to pray about it."

He reached down and grasped both of her hands and gave them a gentle squeeze. "I'm not very good at praying out loud. I have so much to think about, I don't know if I could construct a coherent sentence right now. I need you to stay and pray with me. I know you'll pray for what is right in God's sight, regardless of what I want to do."

"Okay."

Mark nudged the door shut with his foot. They both bowed their heads and began to pray. Chantelle prayed for God to move Mark's heart in the direction that would give God the most glory. She also prayed for a direction that would also be good and pleasing to Mark. When she stopped talking, she didn't pull away. Even though she doubted Mark would pray out loud, she knew he would pray silently, and, therefore, she would continue to pray with him. She didn't have to hear him to know what he was praying. He was praying for exactly the same things she had said, in his own way and wording.

In the silence, her own prayers drifted to questions about the relationship between herself and Mark and how much it had changed since they first met four short months ago. Whether or not he went back to S&B, in less than a month, he was going to leave Aidleyville, and she probably wouldn't see him again.

The realization made her head spin and her stomach churn. In that moment, she realized she loved him. She didn't want him to go, although she had no good reason for him to stay.

He gave her hands a gentle squeeze. "Amen," he mumbled.

"Amen," she replied.

He let her go, but instead of stepping back, his hands drifted to around her back, and he pulled her in close to him. "I'll never forget the way you hugged me after my phone call with Sean. I need a hug from you now more than ever."

It wouldn't have taken any convincing on her part. Chantelle snuggled into his chest, wrapped her arms around his back, and held him tight.

He hadn't held her for more than fifteen seconds when one hand moved. She thought it odd being in a one-armed hug, but suddenly she felt one of the clips being loosened from her hair, followed by another, then another. One by one, she heard the clicks of plastic on metal as they landed on the desk. As soon as the last one was out, his hand returned to her back, and he buried his face in her hair.

"I like that shampoo you use," he muttered.

She tried not to tremble. She wanted him to do more than kiss the top of her head.

Brittany's voice blared over the intercom. "Call for you on line one, Mark."

The harsh interruption made both of them flinch and separate, even though Brittany obviously couldn't see them.

Mark gave her a shaky smile, then turned toward the phone. "Can you take a message, please?" he called out, turning back to Chantelle. He shuffled closer, so they were mere inches apart, and cupped her face in his palms. "I've got a lot to think about. But for now, all I can think about is this."

Before Chantelle realized what he was going to do, Mark lowered his head and brushed a short kiss across the surface of her lips. When she didn't move away, he smiled, embraced her fully, and kissed her again. Slowly, and like he meant it.

Chantelle kissed him back the same way because she meant it, too.

Brittany's voice once again blared over the intercom. "Mark? Call for you on line one. I think it's the same guy."

Chantelle could feel his reluctance as they released each other and separated. "Sorry, I guess I'd better take it. Please come and say good-bye to me before you go home. If we miss each other, I guess I'll see you at lunchtime tomorrow."

All Chantelle could do was nod as she backed up and wrapped her hand around the doorknob.

Mark hit the flashing button on the phone as he sank into the chair. "Mark Daniels," he said, his voice much lower than usual. He cleared his throat, bringing his pitch back to normal. "How can I help you?"

"Mark, this is Stan. I got your message. It seems we made a

mistake on your order. I'm really sorry. I'm holding a truck at the back door. We can make the switch right now, pending your confirmation."

As Mark called up the order on the computer, Chantelle shuffled out of the room. Mark had work to do, and for the next half-hour, she did, too.

And when that half-hour was up, she intended to go home as fast as she could without getting a ticket.

Like Mark, she had some serious praying to do, too. Except now another complication had been added.

No matter what happened, in thirty days, a part of her heart was going to be ripped away, and there was nothing she could do about it.

☙

The next two weeks passed in a blur. Despite their busy schedules, Chantelle spent every minute she could with Mark. She didn't care that on her day off during the week, the employees thought it strange that she spent most of it in the office with Mark.

On his midweek day off, Mark also came to the diner for a major portion of the day, except they couldn't spend the time in the office. He stayed at the front, joking and teasing the servers as he took a few turns at hosting, just so he could spend more time talking to Chantelle, although being at the front lacked the privacy they had in the office.

There were even times when Chantelle didn't do most of the talking.

However, of all the things they talked about, they didn't mention his imminent departure.

With the end of the summer came the end of the tourist season. Mark's research indicated the diner would experience a slump, but that didn't happen. Not only were they busy, they were busier than usual with a busload of seniors having decided to take a week's vacation in Aidleyville for reasons Chantelle couldn't figure out. Other small cities were closer to the coast if people wanted to vacation near the ocean, and other cities had attractions tourists were more likely to find interesting. Even the shopping was geared more to the residents of their small town rather than the transient tourist population.

Chantelle considered their choice of Joe's Diner for mealtime a blessing in disguise because, not only was it good for business, but being so busy gave her less time to dwell on the inevitable fact that Mark was leaving soon.

The day after the merry group departed, Chantelle received a message that Uncle Joe wanted her and Mark to take a few hours off and come to the house so they could talk.

Chantelle knew the day was coming, but to be told it had actually arrived made her stomach churn and her heart pound. She had less than a week, and Uncle Joe and Jack would be back. This was the day Uncle Joe would tell her if she still had a job on Monday.

Chantelle started to count the minutes until she would once again have to see Mark to the airport. Only this time, he would really be getting on the plane.

As they pulled into Uncle Joe's driveway, she was surprised to see Jack's car parked on the street. When they entered the house, Jack and Uncle Joe were sitting on the couch; Susan and Aunt Ellen were in the kitchen chatting.

Uncle Joe motioned them both to sit on the loveseat. "As you know, my doctor has given me a clean bill of health to return to the diner on Monday and the same with Jack. I don't think I have to tell you that my little brush with death has made me think a little differently about things. One of them is that I've spent all my life working in the diner, away from Ellen. I haven't been spending enough time with the person most special to me. I'm close to retirement; I've made a comfortable living. We have money waiting to be spent, so we're going to retire and spend it. I asked Jack to buy me out."

Chantelle gasped and pressed her hands to her cheeks. Next to her, Mark flinched. She glanced quickly at Jack, then to

Mark, then back to Jack again. Jack was a good and fair man, but he wasn't related to her, and he owed her nothing except her salary for time already worked. No doubt, Jack had friends or family of his own he would prefer to have work for him, not a clumsy server with a higher breakage ratio than anyone else in the restaurant industry.

Jack met her eyes. "It seems Joe beat me to the punch. I've been doing a lot of thinking, too, right along the same lines, especially since my leg is never going to be the way it was. I was going to ask Joe to buy me out. I'm ready to retire and start traveling, too."

Chantelle's head reeled. She sat, unable to speak.

Beside her, Mark cleared his throat. "What does this mean?"

Both men looked at each other, then back to Chantelle and Mark.

"It means that Joe's Diner is officially going to be put up for sale tomorrow. We just thought we should tell you privately before we tell the rest of the staff."

"For sale?" she sputtered.

Jack nodded. "Don't worry. Everyone's jobs are still secure. We'll go back to normal on Monday, and we'll run things the way we have been for years until we find a buyer. We're going to make it a condition of sale that no jobs are compromised, unless anyone wants to quit, of course. So don't worry, your job is safe if you want it."

Jack addressed Mark. "I guess you're free to go home now, Mark. Your mom told me they offered you your old job back with a raise attached. I don't know how we can ever thank you for what you've done."

"It was nothing," he mumbled. "Running half of the diner was a life experience I'll never forget." He turned to Chantelle, and their eyes locked. She couldn't read what was in his big brown eyes. Sadness? Regret?

Whatever it was, she was sure her eyes showed the same thing to him.

Chantelle stood and turned away to keep from bursting into tears. "I guess we'd better get back to the diner, then."

Mark stood as well. "Yes. Thanks for letting us know before everyone else. Congratulations on your decision. I know it came with much prayer and careful consideration."

Jack and Uncle Joe stood in unison. "Yes, it was a difficult decision, but we both believe it's the right one."

The return trip to the diner was made in complete silence, which Chantelle didn't consider a bad thing. She didn't think she could speak if her life depended on it.

They walked into the diner to see very few people seated, being the middle of the afternoon on a weekday.

Chantelle expected simply to run down to the lunchroom to retrieve her book, but Mark grabbed her hand and pulled her along behind him. Barely slowing his pace, he spoke as he passed Brittany. "Chantelle and I need to have a meeting before she goes home for the day. Please hold my phone calls."

The second the office door closed, before she had time to sit down, Mark turned around and stood in front of Chantelle, so close that they stood toe to toe. "What do you think?"

"Think? I'm in utter shock. And besides that, I'm obviously going to be out a job soon. I'm a horrible server."

He reached up and cupped her cheeks the same way he had done a couple of weeks ago. Chantelle's head swam.

"They didn't say anything about you serving. They said things would remain the same as they are right now. And right now, you're opening up, hosting, supervising, and doing the cash. Could you do that on an ongoing basis?"

"Of course I could. I didn't think I'd like working in a restaurant, and sometimes it's hard being on my feet all day, but I really like this job."

"And what about me?" he murmured. His thumbs started brushing her cheeks, along her temples, stalling any reasonable thinking process.

"Well. . .I like you, too," she choked out, unable to tell him how she really felt. Whether or not she had a job on Monday, Mark was leaving. In fact, even if she did have a job on Monday, she didn't know how she would still be able to work at the diner without him there. She could picture herself breaking into tears in the middle of seating new patrons—something the new owners would not appreciate.

"I feel the same way," he said as his lips descended on hers.

Fool that she was, she kissed him back in equal measure.

Brittany's voice blared through the intercom. "I'm sorry to interrupt, but we have a problem. A whole busload of teens from the high school just came in for their scheduled tour of the restaurant for career day. My calendar says they're not supposed to be here until tomorrow. Mark, can you show them around?"

Chantelle could feel the regret as Mark pulled away. He cleared his throat. "I'll be there in a minute."

Chantelle ran her fingers through her hair in a futile attempt to straighten it. "I better help Brittany. I guess I'll see you later."

Mark opened the door. "Count on it," he said over his shoulder and walked away.

❧

Chantelle had barely punched in the code for the alarm when she heard the door open again. "Kevin? Is that you? You're early."

Mark appeared behind her. "Nope. It's me."

Her heart pounded in her chest. "What are you doing here so early?"

"We have to talk, and we have to talk right away." He led her to the closest table, where they sat down. "I didn't sleep all night. I spent the whole night praying and thinking. You know they're putting the restaurant up for sale today."

"As if I could forget."

"What do you think about us forming a partnership and running the restaurant on a permanent basis? I think we could do it. You like it, I like it, and we've been doing really well. Profits are up, and we've even hired a couple of extra part-timers. I would like us to own the diner."

Chantelle's heart dropped to somewhere below the bottoms of her shoes. It was almost painful to admit what she had to say. "You know I'm not in a position to do that. I can barely make my rent, never mind come up with a deposit."

He reached across the table and covered her hands with his. "I didn't mean it that way. Remember when we first started this and I said I wasn't asking you to marry me? I've changed my mind. Not only am I asking you to be my permanent part-ner in this business, I'm asking if you'll be my partner for life. I love you, Chantelle. Will you marry me?"

Chantelle's heart stopped, then started up in double time. "Marry you? And run the diner, too? Are you serious? You mean you think we can work together all day and then be together. . .at night?"

He grinned. "I think that's the way it works."

Chantelle looked around her at the so-far empty restaurant she'd come to know and love, then at the man she'd come to love even more.

She grinned back. "It might work."

"Might?"

"Okay, it will work. Of course, I'll marry you. Are you really going to buy the diner? You have enough money for that?"

He nodded. "Not only was that a decent last check from S&B, remember I've done nothing but work for the past three years with no time off. We'll just say I've got some substan-tial savings, plus I've got a few good investments I can cash in. Yes, I can buy the diner."

A tinkle sounded, signifying the main door opening. Mark stood as Kevin and Brittany's voices drifted through the main area of the restaurant, getting louder as they drew closer, then softer as they headed downstairs.

Chantelle couldn't hold back her grin. She stuck out one hand toward him over top of the table. "We'd better shake on it. Partners?"

Mark grinned right back and reached toward her. He grabbed her hand, but didn't return the handshake. Instead, he pulled her to her feet. Once she was standing, he wrapped both hands around her waist and pulled her close. She could feel him smiling as he kissed her.

When they separated, he was still smiling. "Great. We're partners. I'm going to phone Sean and tell him I can't accept that job. Then, I'm going to let Uncle Jack and Joe know I've got a deposit for them. But first, about that next promotional. . ."

He took a step back, tilted his head slightly, and crossed his arms over his chest. "Instead of a turkey contest, what would you think if our next contest featured a wedding theme?"

A Letter To Our Readers

Dear Reader:

In order that we might better contribute to your reading enjoyment, we would appreciate your taking a few minutes to respond to the following questions. We welcome your comments and read each form and letter we receive. When completed, please return to the following:

Fiction Editor
Heartsong Presents
PO Box 719
Uhrichsville, Ohio 44683

1. Did you enjoy reading *Joe's Diner* by Gail Sattler?
   ❑ Very much! I would like to see more books by this author!
   ❑ Moderately. I would have enjoyed it more if

   _____

   _____

   _____

2. Are you a member of **Heartsong Presents**? ❑ Yes ❑ No
   If no, where did you purchase this book? _____

   _____

3. How would you rate, on a scale from 1 (poor) to 5 (superior), the cover design? _____

4. On a scale from 1 (poor) to 10 (superior), please rate the following elements.

   ____ Heroine   ____ Plot
   ____ Hero   ____ Inspirational theme
   ____ Setting   ____ Secondary characters

5. These characters were special because?_____

_____

_____

6. How has this book inspired your life?_____

_____

_____

7. What settings would you like to see covered in future
   Heartsong Presents books? _____

_____

_____

8. What are some inspirational themes you would like to see
   treated in future books? _____

_____

_____

9. Would you be interested in reading other **Heartsong
   Presents** titles? ❑ Yes ❑ No

10. Please check your age range:
     ❑ Under 18   ❑ 18-24
     ❑ 25-34   ❑ 35-45
     ❑ 46-55   ❑ Over 55

Name_____

Occupation _____

Address _____

City_____ State_____ Zip_____

Blind Dates

Mix four single women and one doting grandmother, and what do you get? Blind dates!

Don't miss these charming stories of reluctant romance, spurred by a grandma who knows God has a perfect love for each of her four granddaughters.

Novella, paperback, 352 pages, 5³/₁₆" x 8"

❤ ❤ ❤ ❤ ❤ ❤ ❤ ❤ ❤ ❤ ❤ ❤ ❤

❤ ❤ ❤ ❤ ❤ ❤ ❤ ❤ ❤ ❤ ❤ ❤ ❤

JHEARTSONG ❤ PRESENTS
Love Stories
Are Rated G!

That's for godly, gratifying, and of course, great! If you love a thrilling love story but don't appreciate the sordidness of some popular paperback romances, **Heartsong Presents** is for you. In fact, **Heartsong Presents** is the only inspirational romance book club featuring love stories where Christian faith is the primary ingredient in a marriage relationship.

Sign up today to receive your first set of four, never-before-published Christian romances. Send no money now; you will receive a bill with the first shipment. You may cancel at any time without obligation, and if you aren't completely satisfied with any selection, you may return the books for an immediate refund!

Imagine. . .four new romances every four weeks—two historical, two contemporary—with men and women like you who long to meet the one God has chosen as the love of their lives. . .all for the low price of $10.99 postpaid.

To join, simply complete the coupon below and mail to the address provided. **Heartsong Presents** romances are rated G for another reason: They'll arrive Godspeed!

YES! Sign me up for Heart❤ng!

NEW MEMBERSHIPS WILL BE SHIPPED IMMEDIATELY!
Send no money now. We'll bill you only $10.99 post-paid with your first shipment of four books. Or for faster action, call toll free 1-800-847-8270.

NAME _____

ADDRESS _____

CITY _____ STATE _____ ZIP _____

MAIL TO: HEARTSONG PRESENTS, P.O. Box 721, Uhrichsville, Ohio 44683
or visit www.heartsongpresents.com